T0267402

JUPITER RISING

JUPITER RISING

GARY D. SCHMIDT

CLARION BOOKS

An Imprint of HarperCollinsPublishers

Clarion Books is an imprint of HarperCollins Publishers.

Jupiter Rising

Library of Congress Control Number: 2023944600
ISBN 978-0-35-865964-8

Typography by Sharismar Rodriguez
24 25 26 27 28 LBC 5 4 3 2 1

First Edition

For Benjamin,
with a father's love

one

A FEW days after his thirty-fourth birthday, Quintus Sertorius decided he was as old as any horse should be—and told us so. He started to go stiff in the joints and kind of rigid along his back. His ears went down. He wouldn't move much when I combed him out. He wouldn't finish the oats in his bin. And mostly he kept his eyes shut, even when I ran my hand along his muzzle and told him what a great horse he was and how much we loved him.

Then he started to hold himself really still, and sometimes he'd whinny and throw his head back with his eyes wide open for a moment, and then he'd breathe heavy and quick.

So my father called Dr. Minter, and he came and stroked Quintus Sertorius and felt along his belly and sides. He took his temperature from his rump. He looked into his mouth. He looked into his eyes. He felt along his belly again. He listened to his heart. Then Dr. Minter said to my father, "Bradley, he's lived a good long life, hasn't he?"

"He has," said my father.

Then Dr. Minter said to me, "You know, Jack, the last good thing you can do for Quintus is take away all the pain."

I nodded. I knew that. I didn't want to know that, but I did.

"I can do it now, if you want. Take away the pain, that is."

My father thought about this for a long time.

"No," he said finally. "It's Jack and me should do it."

Dr. Minter nodded.

That afternoon, my father took the tractor and backhoed out a corner in the Far Pasture where Quintus Sertorius had loved to stand with his face up to the cool breezes that came out from the pine trees. He could stand there for an hour or more, sometimes reaching down to chomp on the short grass, but mostly just smelling the piney air. In winter, it was the one spot in the pasture always free from snow, even though big drifts would gather around it. In early April—like right now— it was the first spot with green grass and purple crocuses.

It was *his* spot.

Back in the Big Barn, Quintus Sertorius's teeth were mostly clenched while my father was doing the backhoeing, but he opened them enough to chew the apples I was giving him. He loved to chew apples. I gave him the last ones from the fall crop, and they were still fresh enough that the juice ran at the sides of his mouth. He kept his eyes closed.

Here are the sounds I will remember forever:

The chomping of his teeth on the apples.

The way he ruffled his muzzle in the bin of new oats, even though he didn't eat any.

The *ch-clump, ch-clump, ch-clump* of his hooves on the barn floor.

The quiet in between all that.

It wasn't so long before my father called, "It's time, Jack," and I led Quintus Sertorius out, and so what if I was crying? My father was too. But I led Quintus Sertorius out, and we walked together to the corner of the Far Pasture, Quintus Sertorius with his eyes mostly closed. He was still chewing at the taste of the apples and sometimes his head pulled up, his nostrils wide, smelling the cooler piney air. And I led him down into the deep hole my father had dug, and then Quintus Sertorius did something he never did: he brought his muzzle around and laid it on my shoulder, lightly. He stood very still. I could feel his stiff whiskers. I could smell his warm apple-y breath.

I kissed Quintus Sertorius on the nose, and then my father said I should go back up to the house.

He waited until I got inside—but I could still hear the shot.

My mother jerked a little when it came, and Jupiter looked up from the blocks she was stacking and knocking down and stacking and knocking down on the kitchen floor.

I picked her up and held her. "Jackie crying?" she said.

I shook my head.

"Jackie crying," she said.

It was a long time before my father came back in, and he sat at the kitchen table, and my mother put her hands on his shoulders and said, "Good old Quintus."

"He knew he was going to leave us," said my father.

My mother leaned down and held him tightly.

"Let's not lose anything else," my father said. "Okay?"

My mother nodded.

I remembered that—"Let's not lose anything else"—when Mrs. Stroud from the State of Maine * Department of Health and Human Services drove into our yard later that afternoon.

I WAS USED to seeing Mrs. Stroud—she'd come a whole lot while we were trying to adopt Jupiter, my foster sister, into our family. She always carried a bag with forms to fill out and applications to mark up and questionnaires to answer and evaluations to write on and stuff like that. She smiled the way Quintus Sertorius used to—mostly teeth. And she smiled a lot, because whenever she came, she told us she was so pleased we were adopting Jupiter. "It feels perfect," she would say. "It feels like a completion. Joseph would be so happy."

And Mrs. Stroud was right: Joseph, who was Jupiter's dad, would have been so happy.

Then Mrs. Stroud would nod like she knew

6

what I was thinking, and she'd show that horsey smile again.

This afternoon, though, no horsey smile.

I was coming out of the Big Barn when her car drove up. I'd just finished cleaning out Quintus Sertorius's stall, and maybe I wasn't looking too good—and not just because of the soiled hay I'd been shoveling.

I probably wasn't smelling too good either— and that *was* because of the soiled hay I'd been shoveling.

She got out. "Hello, Jack. Is eighth grade still being kind to you?"

"I guess," I said.

She looked at me. "Are you all right?" she said.

"We put Quintus Sertorius down this morning," I said.

"Oh, Jack, I'm so sorry."

I nodded.

"He'd lived a long life, hadn't he?"

Nodded again.

"But that doesn't matter right now, does it?"

"Not really," I said.

She put her left arm around me—which sort of surprised me because of the way I smelled. In her other hand she was clutching the papers she always carried.

"More forms to sign?" I said. "Last ones?"

She waited a moment. "Can we go up to the house?"

But my mother was already by the open back door, watching.

We went into the kitchen and Mrs. Stroud bent down to pick up Jupiter, who had a block in each hand and was banging them together. "Hello, precious," she said, and she rubbed noses with Jupiter—who always thought rubbing noses was spectacularly funny. Jupiter laughed her high laugh and rubbed noses again.

"Um . . . Jack," said my mother.

"I know."

And I was about to head upstairs to change when Mrs. Stroud said, "Actually, Jack, I wonder

8

if you would like to take Jupiter outside to play for a few minutes."

So I put Jupiter on my back—she never minded the way I smelled—and she said "Horsey?" and we galloped outside. I didn't want to take her into the Big Barn, so we horseyed it up around the Far Pasture and went into the high pines, where there was still a thin and crisp layer of snow on the ground. Immediately the air cooled—it was only early April, so the air could cool quite a lot—and sounds dropped away, and the air tanged with the sticky amber sap, and Jupiter began to laugh when I let the softest lower branches rub against her face.

"Jackie!" she said. She hid her face behind my head. "Jackie!"

I slid her to the ground and she ran from tree to tree, her hands held out and getting stickier and stickier as she grabbed at the trunks, trying to hide from me but giving everything away with her laugh and the crunching snow.

"I'm hiding!" she said.

"I know," I said.

"Jackie can't see me," she said.

"Jackie will always know where you are," I said.

"I know," she said, and more laughing, and more hiding behind trunks too thin to hide much.

And when she got a little tired, she held up her arms and I put her on my back again. She rubbed her sappy hands in my hair. "Jackie's hair is all sticky!"

"I know," I said.

"All sticky," she said, and she laughed and laughed and reached round to try to rub noses.

I carried her past the Far Pasture and up to the ridge above it, where the granite outcroppings had warmed and were showing their bones, and from there higher to the next ridge, where on a clear day you can look up and see three mountain ranges, one behind the other—and you can look down and see the silver Alliance River like a chain necklace, winding its way through granite ledges and pine stands and low blueberry fields and past the quiet graveyard where most of my family slept, including Jupiter's dad, who had slept there for a year and two months. Now I was just about the same age as he would always be, I thought.

"Jackie crying?" said Jupiter.

"No."

Jupiter took hold of my ears and turned my head toward her.

"Jackie crying."

"Because you got my hair all sticky, you goonie-pie."

"I am not a goonie-pie."

"You are a goonie-pie."

"Am not, Jackie."

"Are so, Jupiter."

"Am not."

"Are so."

And that's what we threw back and forth all the way down the ridges, and past the pines, and across the Far Pasture, and by the Big Barn and the Small Barn, and around front of the house, where Mrs. Stroud's car was already gone, and my father's pickup too.

I knelt and Jupiter dropped. "Let's go wash your sticky hands, Jupiter goonie-pie."

"Wash *your* sticky hands, Jackie goonie-pie."

We headed into the kitchen, where my mother stood by the counter. Just stood there, as if she was about to do something with the bag of flour she was holding, but looking like she had forgotten she was holding it.

"Jackie is a goonie-pie," yelled Jupiter.

And my mother dropped the flour to the counter, then dropped herself to one knee, and she held out her hands and Jupiter flew into them and they both rounded their arms around each other and squeezed and squeezed. I watched them. They looked like they would never, ever let go—and not just because Jupiter's hands were so sticky.

JOSEPH WAS JUPITER'S father.

He was also my foster brother, sort of.

He had my back, and I had his.

Since he'd died, I'd missed him like anything.

Like anything.

When we started to foster his daughter, Jupiter, it was like—like I could see sunlight again.

Like I could start to breathe again without hurting so much.

Like there was a reason to breathe again, even if it still did hurt.

That first day, carrying Jupiter into our house, carrying her up to her new room while she held my ears and turned my head so she could rub noses, seeing her climb onto the yellow-quilted bed and find Affy-Giraffey with its long stiff legs and polka-dot bow tie on her pillow—you can't even imagine.

I'm not sure what I would have done, after Joseph died, if Jupiter hadn't come to us.

WHAT I SAID to Mrs. Stroud about eighth grade being kind—that wasn't exactly true.

A few weeks into last December, Coach Swieteck stopped me after one of his I'm-going-to-make-you-run-in-the-frigid-cold-until-you-drop PE classes, and he said he'd been watching me do laps around the track and he thought I might do as a cross-country runner next fall.

I told him I didn't think so.

"Who cares what you think?" he said. "I'm telling you what I see, and I see a runner that might be second or third on JV. Maybe, by the end of the season, fifth on varsity."

"I don't really like to run that much," I said.

He looked at me.

"Oh," I said. "You're not really interested in what I like."

"Not at all," he said.

"So, if I did decide to—"

"I'm going to run you like a dog the rest of eighth grade. And once you're up to pace, I'm going to put you with some of the JV guys in the high school. You're going to run in the summer

14

with them too. Maybe with Jay Perkins. After that, we'll see if I was right."

"Not Jay Perkins."

He looked at me again. "You don't have great short-term memory, do you?"

"You know, Coach, is this because—"

"Hurd, this is because I want a high school cross-country team that will take us to State. That's what this is about."

We looked at each other a long time.

"Okay," I said.

"Go get changed," he said.

I think the first few weeks of me running, Coach Swieteck thought he'd made a really bad decision. I stunk. And it didn't matter why. I just stunk.

While I ran, he hollered, "Hurd, you look like you have flat feet!"

"Hurd, you look like you just got off a horse!"

"Hurd, you look like you haven't taken a dump in three days!"

That sort of stuff.

And he was probably right. I probably did look like that.

But then my parents told me on a cold, cold, cold night in February that it finally looked like we'd be able to adopt Jupiter, and she would live with us permanently. It would still take a while— the State had to finish investigating the families of both her parents, and so far, no one had been able to find Joseph's mother. But the time allowed for those investigations would elapse soon, and it was pretty sure: we'd be able to adopt her.

We finally would.

And everything changed.

Everything.

After the next run, Coach Swieteck said, "That's more like it."

The run after that, Coach Swieteck said, "Someone turn a switch on for you?"

The run after that, Coach Swieteck said, "I suppose that will do for now."

The run after that, Coach Swieteck said, "You

might give Jay Perkins a run for his money."

"I don't want to run with Jay Perkins," I said.

"Yeah," said Coach Swieteck. "When I told him he was going to be one of your partners, he said he didn't want to run with you either."

"So what did you say to him then?"

"What do you think I said to him then, Hurd?"

"That you weren't really interested in what he wanted."

Coach Swieteck waved toward the track. "Take another lap to cool down."

two

WHEN something as good as Jupiter coming into our family happens, it touches everything.

And not just cross-country so Coach Swieteck could have a team that could go to State.

My other teachers noticed too.

Mrs. Halloway—she taught eighth-grade Language Arts—said she noticed that I wasn't looking out the window as much when we discussed *Of Mice and Men*. She wondered if I had finally been completely caught up by Steinbeck's evocative language.

I let her go ahead and think that.

Mr. Collum, who taught eighth-grade Science, said I was getting a whole lot better at lab reports. "Not that you'd have to do very much to improve upon what you've been handing in so far. Even a modicum of effort would do that."

He could be sort of a jerk sometimes.

"What's your next project?" he said.

I told him that my next project was going to be on inherited genes. I was going to use my brother as an example.

"Weren't you both adopted?" he said.

"My brother and his daughter, Jupiter," I said. "They both have black hair and black eyes."

He waited a while, and then he said, "Okay, Jack. That could work."

He wasn't always a jerk.

Mr. D'Ulney, who taught Algebra, said my first semester as an eighth-grade mathematician showed pretty clearly that I did not have the mathematical instincts of my brother, but after he saw my enthusiasm in these last few weeks, he was more confident that I'd be able to get by in life arithmetically.

He could be sort of a jerk sometimes too, but he had been Joseph's favorite teacher, so . . .

And Ms. Uchida, who taught Music, said she had been wondering most of the school year if I would ever understand the concept of pitch. She had never run into anybody who couldn't, she said, but she'd almost come to the conclusion that I was, indeed, completely "pitch-proof." However, in these last few days, she believed I had proven that I could still sing with a "zest" that was acceptable. Perhaps someday I'd be in a church choir? In the back row?

I told her it was more likely that Rosie and Dahlia—our cows—would be singing duets at

First Congregational before I would be singing in a choir.

"You never know," said Ms. Uchida, and she smiled.

Anyway, that's how things changed after we started to adopt Jupiter.

By the way, that very first night, after my parents told me we were going to adopt her, you know who I went to tell first, right?

It had snowed during the day, one of those light late winter snows when every flake is sort of pillowy. By suppertime there was maybe three or four inches on the ground, not so much. And then the full moon came out, and while the sky was ink black and the snow was milk white, I walked through the Far Pasture—every snowflake a lit diamond—and then over the granite ledges and past the pine stands that laid their blue shadows across the white drifts, and then through the low blueberry fields where the snow had collected up to my shins, all the way to the Hurd family graveyard. Our stones go back almost three hundred years, and there are a lot of them, mostly scattered around. The oldest are slate and pretty chipped and worn down, but the new ones are shiny and still sharp, and they threw shadows on the snow darker than the pines.

I put my hands on Joseph's gravestone. The polished granite was warm. Really, it was. I don't know why. But it was warm.

"Joseph," I said. "Joseph, listen. We're adopting Jupiter. Really. Just what you wanted. It will take a while, but she'll live here. With us. She'll grow up on the farm. She'll milk Rosie like you did. And maybe she'll ride Quintus Sertorius except he's getting old and fidgety so he might not let people ride on him much longer. We'll be her family. I'll tell her all about you. And I promise, Joseph, I'll always know where she is. Do you hear that? I promise."

It was really quiet after that. I mean, *really* quiet. No wind. Not even an owl. But not spooky at all. While I climbed up the ridge toward home,

I felt the weight of the moon's warm silver hands on my back, like Jupiter was already riding there.

Or maybe the hands were Joseph's.

IT WAS ONLY a few days after Quintus died that Coach Swieteck gave me the okay to run with the JV. I guess he told the JV runners too, because I got a text from Jay Perkins that told me to wait at the end of the road to our farmhouse on Monday afternoon and don't be late. I had a dream about them the night before. It was horrible. Jay Perkins was in the lead. Behind him came two thugs: Nick Porter and Brian Boss. They were screaming "You're dead, kid" as they sprinted toward me, and from somewhere I heard Joseph hollering, "Don't let them get behind you," but they were circling me now and Nick Porter got behind me and I was slamming Jay Perkins into lockers that had suddenly appeared on the road and I was about to scream when I woke up.

And I heard it again, even though I was awake:

"Don't let them get behind you."

That was the dream.

So I was stretching at the end of our road, waiting for my running partners. And of course, when they showed, Jay Perkins was in the lead, and behind him came Nick Porter and Brian Boss.

No kidding.

It would have been funny if it wasn't so horrible, since Porter and Boss were snarling and sneering and really did look like thugs who were going to rip my head off.

Jay Perkins was way in the lead—he must have been sprinting the last quarter mile before he got to me—and he bent over and put his hands on his knees, face down to catch his breath. When he got it, he stood up, swung his bright yellow stocking cap behind his back, put his hands on his hips, looked at me, and said, "Just so you know, I'm only doing this because Coach said I had to."

"Me too," I said.

"It's not something I want to do."

"Me either."

I should tell you, Jay Perkins is a lot bigger than me. If we stood back to back, my head wouldn't reach his shoulders. His arms are long, and right now at their ends were clenched hands, like he was ready to pound me—which he probably was. And he already had kind of a mustache, for crying out loud.

He stretched his arms up behind his head. "I can't freaking believe Coach is making me do this."

I waited. What was I supposed to say?

Nick Porter and Brian Boss came up, and they stood like two bears, their eyes half closed, looking like they were going to eat me after they ripped my head off.

"Sugar," said Nick Porter. (He didn't really say "Sugar"—but, you know.)

Brian Boss nodded his head. "Yeah. Sugar." (Not really "Sugar" from Brian Boss either.)

I figured that they'd each just used up half of their vocabulary.

"So, listen," said Jay Perkins. "We're not baby-ing you. We're training for varsity tryouts next fall, and running with a pathetic eighth grader is a waste of time."

"Yeah," said Brian Boss.

"So we come by here at four o'clock every day. You be out here, stretched and ready to go."

"Okay."

"If you're not here, or if you're not ready, don't expect us to wait."

"I won't."

"Because we won't."

"I get it."

"And this is just Monday through Friday. Not weekends."

I nodded.

"And we're not running *together*. You get that too? We're not running together. I don't care what Coach says."

"So how—"

"You stay back. Fifty feet, maybe."

"So how do I know when we change the pace?"

Long pause. "Just watch my ass, idiot. If it's disappearing from view, then you're too slow. Dang, I hate this. Are those the shoes you're running in?"

I nodded.

"You get that those aren't running shoes?"

I looked at them. "I know."

"They're for, like, basketball or something. Not running."

"Okay."

"Sugar," said Nick Porter. (Not really.)

Jay Perkins looked at him, then back at me. "I so hate this. Are you ready? One loop with us. You get it? One loop. Then you peel off."

We set out.

I think they were all sprinting, because soon they did pretty much disappear from view. I ran about a mile and finally saw Jay Perkins waiting up ahead, the bears panting nearby, and Jay Perkins spoke the last words he said to me that day: "Keep the hell up."

Lovely.

I tried, but they were all a whole lot better than me, and I watched Jay Perkins's stupid bright yellow stocking cap (I wasn't going to watch his ass) swing across his back as the three of them drew away until they were far enough in front that no one who saw us could have imagined we were actually running together—which I guess was the point.

They disappeared entirely from view a couple more times, like when they ran down Sumner Hill Road, and when they ran up Jefferson Hill Road, and when they turned through Jenny's Notch, and when they crossed Mill Road along the Alliance River. But I always managed to catch up, even when they sprinted up Sumner Hill Road to complete the loop.

Ahead of me, they reached the turnoff to my house, and I couldn't tell if they slowed down or not. Probably not. They just ran on and I stopped, breathing like Quintus Sertorius after a gallop, and I watched the three of them head down Sumner Hill Road again for another loop, like they could be doing this without stopping forever.

I think I might have hated their guts right then.

When I got back inside, my mother asked if I'd enjoyed running with my partners on our first day.

"It was great," I said.

I went upstairs and collapsed on my bed.

The next day, Coach Swieteck asked how it went.

"Fine," I said.

"Perkins said you don't have what it takes."

"I was in a fight with Jay Perkins once. I won."

"If I heard that story right, you smashed into his back, Hurd."

"Yeah. I smashed his face into the lockers. And I won."

"That's not how he tells it."

"What a surprise," I said.

Coach Swieteck came closer. "So show him you have what it takes."

I wasn't sure I could.

They were back the next day at four o'clock,

and I was stretched and ready. They didn't say hello. They didn't nod. They didn't even look at me. I just fell in behind them—fifty feet behind them—and stayed within sight of Jay Perkins's stupid bright yellow stocking cap.

They never looked back, the jerks.

Not once.

But if they had, they would have seen me—because after that first day, I never lost sight of them again. If I had had to run barefoot on gravel, if I had had to crawl on glass with bloody knees, if I had had to sprint on fiery coals, I would not have lost sight of them.

They ran past the turnoff to my house to finish the loop, and I stopped there, breathing to try to get air, any air, into my lungs, and I watched Jay Perkins's stocking cap disappear down Sumner Hill Road.

And as soon as I knew they were gone, I went over to the side of the road and threw up.

So what?

Lots of people throw up after they run.

But that's pretty much how it went the first week we ran together.

Keep them in sight, keep them in sight, keep them in sight, throw up.

And that's pretty much how it went the second week too—until Friday.

Because on Friday—even though I was breathing like anything to get some air into my lungs, and even though I was ready to throw up again—after Jay Perkins and Nick Porter and Brian Boss ran past the turnoff to my house, I did too.

Sprinting.

Closing the gap to a lot less than fifty feet.

When he heard me, Jay Perkins turned around to look back.

He took off his stupid bright yellow stocking cap and held it in his hand.

He picked up the pace.

Nick Porter and Brian Boss did too.

Down Sumner Hill Road, up Jefferson Hill Road, through Jenny's Notch, across Mill Road, and up Sumner Hill Road to complete the second loop.

And this time, while Nick Porter and Brian Boss ran on, Jay Perkins waited at the end of the turnoff.

I staggered up to him. I really, really, really needed to breathe.

I also really, really, really needed to throw up.

"You know, Hurd, I could have taken you apart that day in the locker room if I'd wanted to."

I nodded.

"Sometimes I still want to."

Nodded again. Then I said, "It was three on one"—breathe breathe breathe—"Joseph"—breathe—"was by himself"—breathe breathe breathe—"until I got there."

"He started it," said Jay Perkins.

"Three on one"—breathe breathe—"I bet"—breathe—"you felt real proud"—breathe— "about that."

"You don't know anything," said Jay Perkins. "And by the way, save your very best stuff for the end of the run, idiot. Don't come in like you're dying—even if you are. Sprint in like you've got what it takes."

Breathe—nod.

Jay Perkins stepped back. I thought he might be going to run after Nick Porter and Brian Boss. But then he said, "Listen, this weekend, just a couple of short runs. Easy pace. Try to control your breathing. And you carry your stupid hands too high. Bring them down lower, like this. And stop bobbling your head around. You look like a jackass."

"Okay," I whispered.

He threw his bright yellow stocking cap into my chest.

"Wear this so you don't get chilled," he said. "Coach would probably make me tuck you into bed if you got sick or something—and you know I'm not going to do that."

He turned and started down Sumner Hill Road.

"Go throw up," he called over his shoulder.

I did.

three

THAT weekend, I did a couple of short runs. Easy pace. My breathing controlled. Hands lower. Head not bobbling.

I wore Jay Perkins's stupid stocking cap.

On Monday afternoon, when I was at the end of our road and all stretched out, Jay Perkins showed up, a new pink stocking cap on his head and a pair of running shoes tied around his neck.

"Put these on," he said. He threw them into me.

"Whose are—"

"My old ones. Now they're yours—if they fit. You can't run in basketball shoes."

I looked at them. It wasn't like they were new, but . . . "Thanks," I said.

"Just put them on," he said.

I did.

"They fit?"

"I guess."

"No, idiot. Run to that rock and back. You have to run in them to see if they fit."

I did.

"They fit fine," I said.

"Then let's go. Stay on my ass this time."

"Where's Porter and Boss?"

"You don't want to know," he said.

I waited.

"Okay, so they told Coach they weren't going to run with an eighth grader anymore, and Coach said they were going to run with an eighth grader if they wanted to try out for varsity next year, and they said maybe they didn't want to try out for varsity that bad, and Coach went into his office, brought out his clipboard, took a red pen, and scratched their names off the varsity list."

"Sugar," I said. (Not really.)

"Yeah. I'd stay away from them if I were you." He turned to run.

"Hey," I said. "How come you're still running with an eighth grader?"

"None of your business," he said. "Stay on my ass."

I did. I stayed right behind him for the first loop, because running in those shoes was like running on a breeze.

For the second loop, pretty close behind him—because it doesn't matter if you're wearing the best running shoes in the world, running when you know you're going to throw up at the end is never like running on a breeze.

· · · · ·

ON TUESDAY, THE bus home was late, and by the time we got to my stop and I ran to the house and I ran upstairs and I got my stuff on and Jay Perkins's shoes and bright yellow stocking cap and banged back downstairs, Jay Perkins was already standing in my kitchen.

He was holding Jupiter.

She was pulling at his new pink stocking cap.

Jupiter was laughing.

My mother was laughing.

Jay Perkins was laughing too.

Jupiter pulled his stocking cap off and dropped it on the floor.

"Hey," said Jay Perkins.

Then Jupiter pulled both his ears.

"Why are you pulling my ears?" said Jay.

Jupiter laughed this high giggle.

She leaned in and rubbed noses with Jay.

Then she saw me, and pointed.

"Funny hat!" she said.

She leaned out toward me and I took her and

she hauled off my stocking cap and threw it on the floor and pulled my ears. "Funny Jackie."

Jay Perkins reached down and picked up his cap. "We'd better get going."

I put down Jupiter and picked up my cap. "See you in a little while, Jupiter."

She blew two kisses toward me. "You too, funny Jackie goonie-pie."

And then Jay Perkins did this strange thing: he leaned over and kissed Jupiter lightly on the forehead. She put her arms around his neck and kissed him back. After that, we went outside and headed down our road at a slow trot.

At Sumner Hill Road, Jay Perkins said, "Don't think I'm always going to come and get you when you're late."

"I know. Sorry."

"You look like a jerk in my hat," he said.

"How do you think you look?"

"Primo," he said, and he started running. "Watch my ass," he called back.

But I didn't. I ran up beside him, and we ran

the two loops together—mostly—until the last part up Sumner Hill Road, when he sprinted and I didn't because I knew what was coming—and then Jay Perkins ran on down Sumner Hill Road. But right before he was out of sight—and right before I did you-know-what—he brought his hand up and waved.

From that day on, Jay Perkins met me in the kitchen—I think so he could hold Jupiter. She would take off his pink stocking cap and throw it on the floor and take him by the ears and rub noses. When I told him he didn't have to come all the way to the house, he said he didn't mind much.

"Really," I said. "I can meet you at—"

"I said it was okay," he said.

"But—"

"Listen, Jackie goonie-pie, you're not the only one who's—"

But he didn't finish. He took off, and I followed. On the run that day, he never quite let me catch up.

That day, he started his sprint up Sumner Hill

Road earlier than he ever had before.

That day, I didn't even try to keep up with him.

But almost every other day, I did keep up with Jay Perkins, and soon I was doing a third lap with him. Down Sumner Hill Road, up Jefferson Hill Road, through Jenny's Notch, across Mill Road, and up Sumner Hill Road again.

And I never could catch Jay Perkins on that last sprint of the loop, but he always waited for me at the top now—probably because Jupiter was usually there with my mother. And when I got up to them, Jay would be holding her and Jupiter would be taking his pink cap off and pulling his ears and Jay Perkins would be laughing. Then he'd put his stocking cap back on and she'd pull it over his eyes and he'd take it off and put it on her and she'd pull it over her eyes and giggle like all get-out.

Then Jay Perkins would hand her over to me and she would pull my stocking cap off and drop it on the ground and grab my ears. Then she'd blow Jay a kiss and he'd blow a kiss back—really, Jay

Perkins did that—and then he'd pull his cap back on and run off, waving at the turn.

A COUPLE OF weeks after I started running with Jay Perkins, Coach Swieteck waited for me by the gym door.

"So how is the running going?"

I shrugged. "Okay, I guess."

"Stop that," he said. "I hate that humble crap. Just tell me, are you getting better or not?"

I nodded.

"Tomorrow afternoon. Three o'clock. Right after school. You'll do two miles—eight laps. Don't be late. I hate eighth graders who think they can make me wait for them."

"Is this, like, a tryout?"

"I'll tell Perkins you won't be running with him tomorrow. And it's to decide if I should waste my time on you or not."

"Coach, I'm not as good as Jay Perkins, you know."

"I already told you what I think of that humble crap, right? And that's the last time I say something to you twice. Got it?"

"Okay," I said. "Got it."

"Now go away. I've got these mats to spread out."

"You want me to help?"

"You think I can't spread some mats out, Hurd? You think I can't do it because I'm in a wheelchair? You think I'm some sort of poor disabled—"

"I didn't mean that."

"You better not mean that. Go away."

The next day I ran the two miles in 12:07.

"Next time, get in under six-minute miles," said Coach Swieteck.

"How much under?" I said.

He looked at me.

"Oh," I said. "That much."

"Take a couple of laps to cool down," Coach Swieteck said.

"Coach, I might miss the bus if I—"

"It's a tough world," said Coach Swieteck, and he headed back inside.

. . . . .

TURNS OUT, COACH Swieteck was right.

On the day we put Quintus Sertorius down and Mrs. Stroud drove up to talk with my parents and Jupiter and I went up to the pine trees by the Far Pasture and my mother stood at the sink holding the bag of flour and Jupiter and I went to wash our sticky hands, my father came back late from town and we ate a pretty quiet supper. Jupiter and I dried dishes while my mother didn't talk. Later, my father played blocks with Jupiter—"Jupe, how high do you think you can build these?"—and she put one on top of another on top of another, and then knocked them down until she was yawning. Then I read three books to her about bunnies because she loved books about bunnies, and my mother picked her up and she patted Jupiter on her back and Jupiter yawned and waved at me, and I said "Good night, Jupiter goonie-pie" and she said "Good night, Jackie goonie-pie" and she laid her head down on my mother's shoulder and closed her eyes and they headed upstairs.

Then my father said, "Jack," and I looked at him.

He looked like he was about to cry.

I stood.

"Jack," he said again. "You know that Mrs. Stroud was here this afternoon."

I waited.

"She had some news for us."

It got really quiet. Like everything everywhere held its breath and closed its eyes and made its hands into fists.

"What kind of news?"

He leaned forward.

"Jack, there's no easy way to tell you this. So here it is: Jupiter's grandparents are demanding custody."

I held my breath and closed my eyes and made my hands into fists.

"What?" I said.

"Jupiter's grandparents want to adopt Jupiter."

"It's too late," I said.

"Not in the state of Maine."

"We already adopted her."

"It's not finalized."

"They didn't want her before. Right? They didn't want her before."

"That's right."

"So why now?"

"They're her closest blood relatives. They get to have a say in what happens to her."

"They don't get to have a say after all this time—"

"Yes they do."

"—just because they're blood relatives. She's living with us. Joseph would want her to live with us. He wanted that. Doesn't he get a say?"

"Not anymore, Jack."

"I promised him I'd always know where she is!"

"I know."

"I promised her too!"

"I know you did, Jack. I know it."

"I freaking promised her."

My father nodded.

I went out of the kitchen. I might have slammed the door.

I went into the Big Barn. Past Quintus Sertorius's freaking empty stall. To the cow stalls.

Rosie mooed when she saw me, and I stood next to her and scratched her rump like Joseph learned to do and she mooed again, and I stayed there until my father came in with a lantern to find me.

"Jack," he said.

"You can't let this happen."

"Jack, I'll try. But—"

"You can't let this happen. Jupiter belongs here. You can't let this happen."

"I can only try."

And then, I did something I never thought I would ever, ever, *ever* do. I hit him across the chest. As hard as I could.

He just stood there and took it.

He just took it.

Then he opened up his arms, and I fell against

him and cried and cried because it was so unfair.
So freaking unfair.

Because I promised her that I would always
know where she was.

And because I promised Joseph that I would
always know where she was.

And because you can't keep losing what you
love most in all the world.

You just can't.

You just freaking can't.

four

LAST February, the warmer days came before they were supposed to, and the sap began to run in the sugar maple trees a little earlier than my father had predicted, so we had to tap ours in a hurry. Jupiter helped us by hanging on to my back and letting me carry her from tree to tree—all seventy of them. My father hammered in the spile, and I bent down and Jupiter grabbed the handle of a pail to hook around it, and I put the cover on the pail, and then I carried her behind my father to the next tree.

Seventy times.

She loved it all: the bright February sky, the hammering, me bending down with her and almost tipping over on purpose until she pulled my ears back, the shiny clean pails, the smell of maples starting to wake up.

And a few days later, when the sap was running like all get-out, she helped haul the pails down to the sugaring shed—which meant that I carried her and one pail down to the sugaring shed.

Seventy times.

It took a while.

Jupiter didn't care.

We hauled the pails into the shed while my father tended the fire under the pans—trying not to laugh when I came in with only one pail and a giggling Jupiter.

Later, she stayed on my back so she could watch the sap boil and get drained from one pan to the next, and the next, and the next, and then darken into syrup. This took a long time too, but Jupiter—like I said—didn't care. Me either, really.

And late one morning, after a really cold night, my father drained some of the syrup and poured it onto a patch of snow, and Jupiter ate it, her eyes big.

And the day after that, my father let some of the syrup boil and boil until it turned into soft sugar, and he cut it into squares and gave a piece to Jupiter, and this time her eyes got even bigger, and she got maple sugar all over her face and all over her hands, and she held her fingers up to us and my father said, "Sticky!" and she laughed and she said "Icky sticky!"—her very first rhyme. And I thought how amazing it would be, how incredibly amazing it would be, to watch Jupiter do everything for the very first time.

Read a book on her own, ride a horse by herself, climb one of the old pines beyond the Far Pasture, milk Rosie without any help, come home from her first day in kindergarten, throw a snowball, skate on the pond where Joseph skated, catch lightning bugs in mason jars on a summer night, and look up into the winter sky and pick out the planet Jupiter rising brighter than any star.

How amazing it would be.

THE NIGHT AFTER Mrs. Stroud told us, when my father and I came in from the barns, we found my mother in the front room, adding some sticks to the wood stove. "Jupiter's asleep," she said.

"She always falls asleep so quickly," said my father.

"She always does," I said.

And that's about all we said for the rest of the night, the three of us in the front room, watching the wood stove, feeling its warm breath. What else was there to say? My father and mother mostly held hands, and I lay on the rag rug in front of the fire with a copy of *Octavian Nothing* that I was reading again—except I wasn't reading it. My mother went out to the kitchen and came back with three mugs of hot chocolate; none of us drank it. The mantel clock chimed nine o'clock, then ten o'clock, and my mother got up to wind it for the week.

"I guess it's time for bed," she said. She started to turn out the light.

But my father leaned forward on the couch. "You know, Jack, one of the things I loved most about Quintus is that he never gave up. You know that. If he was pulling out a stump, or hauling a load of stones out of the fields, or dragging the sledge through heavy snow, he never gave up."

My father stood and walked over to the stove. He threw in some lengths of wood and pulled the damper closed. The room was mostly dark.

"I don't know how this is going to end. Jupiter's grandparents have lots of money to spend, and it sounds like they're used to getting whatever they want. We don't even have the money to pay for what a lawyer would cost. But . . ."

"Let's never give up," I said.

"Let's never give up," he said back.

And I'm not just telling a story here, but at that moment, the clouds broke and the full moon threw everything it had at our house. It beamed into the window and flooded us with silver light so bright that my mother gasped.

IF YOU LIVE in a small town like East Sumner, you get used to everyone knowing everything that's going on all around you. And you get used to knowing that everyone knows your business, but no one talks about it—which makes things weird sometimes.

So when the bus passed on the way to school the next morning, every face was at the window, staring at me. Then when I got to school, John Wall, Danny Nations, and Ernie Hupfer were sitting on the front steps, and they surrounded me and walked in with me and didn't say anything.

It felt good.

In Language Arts, Mrs. Holloway touched me

on the shoulder during silent reading. We were done with *Of Mice and Men*—which was pretty sad—and on to *Cry, the Beloved Country*, which you just knew was going to end badly too. So maybe she thought I needed some distraction or something.

Anyway, that's how Mrs. Halloway told me she knew.

In Science, we spent the lab hour distilling a concentrate into aspirin. Mr. Collum put me with Danny Nations as a lab partner, which was great because Danny Nations was someday going to win the Nobel Prize in Chemistry and my usual lab partner was Rowley Anderson, who was someday going to win the Nobel Prize in Getting Out of Work and Making Your Lab Partner Do Everything.

That's how Mr. Collum told me he knew.

In Algebra, Mr. D'Ulney stopped me after class and gave me a folder filled with geometric proofs. "I was going to keep these," he said, "but I thought you might like to have them instead." The proofs were ones that Joseph had done, all written out in the neat small letters that Joseph used, all on blank paper but in perfectly straight lines, all ending with a QED—which he'd written in the largest letters of all, as if he was asking you to admire how terrific the proofs were.

That's how Mr. D'Ulney told me he knew.

And in Music, Ms. Uchida left me and the whole tenor section alone. We were terrible, but she didn't make us go over and over and over the lyrics—even though we really, really stunk.

That's how Ms. Uchida told me she knew.

And Coach Swieteck made me and John Wall run laps while everyone else suffered through stupid apparatus stuff. "You don't talk while I talk," he said to John, who was chatting a tiny bit in his squad—like everybody else. "Take some laps. Hurd, you pace him. Seven-minute miles. Get out of here."

That's how Coach Swieteck told me he knew.

Mr. Canton, the vice principal, knew too.

He saw me in the hall and told me to follow him to his office. When we got there, he closed the door.

"I heard about what's going on with Jupiter," he said.

"Yeah," I said.

"You know, Hurd, I used to warn you about hanging around with Joseph Brook."

"I remember."

"I told you he'd get you into trouble. I told you I knew kids like him and they were bad news."

I waited.

"And you know what? I was wrong. Well, kind of wrong. He'd get you into trouble—you know I'm right about that, Jack. But I think he was the kind of kid that would always get you out of trouble too, wasn't he?"

"He had my back," I said.

"I believe it. The thing is, are you going to have his now?"

I looked at him. "What do you mean?"

"I mean, you're going to have to fight like heck to keep his daughter where she belongs. You ready for that?"

I leaned forward. "I am," I said.

He leaned toward me. "Good," he said. He wrote something down on a pad, ripped off the page, and handed it to me. "My sister is a lawyer over to Augusta. Tell your parents to call her. She'll take this on. No charge."

"No charge?"

"Tell them she's waiting for their call."

I tucked the paper into my backpack.

"Mr. Canton," I said, "why are you doing this?"

He smiled—not really a vice principal smile. "I owe a favor to Joseph Brook, and I'm remembering to pay the debt."

I looked at him.

"Just tell them to call her."

I TOLD THEM to call, and they did, and Miss Canton set up a meeting, and that was all good.

But you know, maybe the universe sometimes tries to pay you back. Maybe it does. Because on one of the worst days of my life, something good happened.

Marcus Aurelius came.

It wasn't like he was a kid. He was ten years old, which is pretty mature for a horse. He was brown with a white star on his forehead and a big white splash across his back. He held his head high, like he was sort of a proud horse. But when Jupiter held an apple out to him, he'd lower his muzzle and take it gently with his big teeth—he was going to remind us of Mrs. Stroud the way Quintus Sertorius had—and then he'd lower his head more so we could scratch him on the poll. He loved being groomed, and when we brushed him, he'd close his eyes with the pleasure of it. He was careful where he put his feet, which was pretty important with Jupiter around. And he made these warm snuffling noises whenever we came into his stall, and he'd swish his long black tail around and around to tell us he was glad to be here with us.

We were glad he was here too.

And even though he was like fifty times as big as Jupiter, she wasn't afraid.

I tried not to be afraid too.

five

ON the first Saturday in May, Mrs. Stroud drove into the yard, which was more than a little muddy—it was that time of year. Mr. and Mrs. Joyce were in the back seat of the car. It was their first court-approved visitation.

It was not a Hurd family—approved visitation, but there was nothing we could do about it, Miss Canton had said.

Jupiter and I were standing by the Small Barn,

where I'd been pushing her on the rope swing my father had hung from one of the beams years ago.

My mother and father came out into the yard.

Mrs. Stroud got out of the car and stood by her door.

Mr. and Mrs. Joyce got out and stood by their doors.

It was pretty still, except that Mr. Joyce was looking down at his shoes, which were shiny but wouldn't be for long.

Jupiter—who wore her green rubber boots— slosh-ran to Mrs. Stroud. "Hello, precious," Mrs. Stroud said. They rubbed noses.

"Jackie is a goonie-pie," said Jupiter.

"I think there may be times when we are all goonie-pies," said Mrs. Stroud.

Jupiter shook her head. "No," she said. "Jackie and Jay!"

Then Mrs. Joyce leaned down and held out her arms. "Hello, Jupiter," she said.

Jupiter walked right into her arms and hugged her, because that's what Jupiter does.

Okay, so maybe I wished she hadn't done that. Maybe I wished Jupiter had picked up a handful of mud and slung it at her. Maybe I wished Jupiter had kicked Mrs. Joyce as hard as she could and Mrs. Joyce had fallen into the mud and then driven off in a huff. Maybe I wished that Jupiter hadn't reached for Mrs Joyce's ears, and that Mrs. Joyce hadn't laughed and let Jupiter turn her head first to the right, then to the left. Maybe I wished that Mrs. Joyce hadn't rubbed noses with Jupiter.

You wouldn't have wanted any of that either.

"You look so much like Madeleine," Mrs. Joyce said.

I walked up to Jupiter and took her hand. "Let's go inside and change your boots," I said. Jupiter went with me, but she turned back and waved to Mrs. Joyce.

I picked her up and carried her up the stairs and into the house. In the mudroom, I took off her green boots. I tied on her sneakers.

"Jackie crying?" she said.

"No, I'm not crying, Jupiter. You always think

61

I'm crying when I'm not."

"It's okay," she said, and she put her arms around my neck and—no kidding—she patted my back.

I carried her into the kitchen.

The Joyces had already come in. They were sitting on one side of the kitchen table. My parents were on the other side. Mrs. Stroud sat at the end. They were all looking like they had to go to the bathroom pretty bad.

But probably Jupiter didn't notice that, since Mrs. Joyce had a white polar bear bigger than Jupiter in her lap. She held it out, and Jupiter ran to the stupid polar bear and buried her face in its white fur.

"It's for you, Jupiter. You mother loved polar bears, and I thought you would like to have one."

Jupiter squeezed the polar bear hard.

I tried not to hope that all the stupid stuffing would come out of its mouth, like it was throwing up or something.

"She already has Affy-Giraffey," I said.

Mrs. Joyce watched Jupiter. She didn't even look at me. "I bet Giraffey isn't as big as this polar bear," she said.

You know how sometimes at the beginning of the school year you walk into your classroom and you see your teacher and right away you know you're going to like her? It isn't always like that, but sometimes it is. I mean, it's the first day of the year, and your teacher has to pretend she's strict or something to convince everyone that they're going to have to listen to her. But you can tell that it's all an act—that she probably really is a pretty nice person and you're going to get along fine.

That's not how it was with Mrs. Joyce.

I knew we wouldn't get along fine.

"*Affy*-Giraffey," I said.

"What do you say, Jupiter?" said my mother.

"Thank you," said Jupiter.

"The polar bear is from your grandfather too," said Mrs. Joyce.

Jupiter carried the polar bear past Mrs. Joyce and stood on her tiptoes to kiss Mr. Joyce's cheek—but when he leaned down, Jupiter reached up and grabbed his left ear.

"Stop that," he said, and sat up.

I think it sort of surprised Jupiter. She turned around and looked at me, and I mouthed, "Thank you."

And she turned back and said "Thank you" to Mr. Joyce.

He nodded. "You're welcome," he said.

"Would you like to show us around the farm?" said Mrs. Joyce.

Jupiter ran across the kitchen and handed me the stupid polar bear. Then she ran back and took Mrs. Joyce's hand.

"It's pretty muddy," said Mr. Joyce.

"I have boots," said Jupiter, and she let go of Mrs. Joyce's hand and ran back to me.

We went to the mudroom again. We stuffed the stupid polar bear into her cubby. She sat down on the bench and I took off her sneakers. I put on her green boots again. She ran out to the kitchen.

They were all still sitting there, still looking

like they had to go to the bathroom pretty bad.

Jupiter ran to Mrs. Joyce, took her hand, and looked back at me. "C'mon, Jackie," she said.

I looked at Mrs. Stroud, who shook her head.

"I'll wait here, Jupiter," I said. "You can show them around. Take them to see your rope swing."

"Jackie, c'mon!"

I shook my head. "I'll be right here."

"Jackie, carry me."

"That would be fine," said Mrs. Joyce. "We won't go far, anyway."

So I carried Jupiter outside.

We started in the Big Barn, and Jupiter pointed to Dahlia, who ignored us as usual, and Rosie, who mooed happily when she saw Jupiter. Then Jupiter led them to Marcus Aurelius's stall. "His name's . . ." She looked back at me.

"Marcus Aurelius," I said.

Marcus Aurelius stamped his foot once and shook his head.

Mr. Joyce asked if the Big Barn always smelled this way.

We went into the Small Barn and Jupiter got down from my back and climbed onto the rope swing. "Push me," she said, and I did.

"Are you sure it's safe?" Mrs. Joyce asked.

Jupiter got onto my back again and we went to the Far Pasture, which was already turning green with the warmer sun.

"Is it always this muddy?" Mr. Joyce asked.

We climbed up the ridge beyond the Far Pasture so they could see the three mountain ranges.

"Does Jupiter ever climb up here alone?" Mrs. Joyce asked.

"Isn't this dangerous?" Mr. Joyce asked.

Jupiter pointed to the graveyard beyond the silver Alliance. "That's where my daddy is asleep," she said.

Mr. and Mrs. Joyce stepped onto the granite of the ridge and looked down.

"That's where your daddy is dead," said Mr. Joyce. He turned to his wife—"and good riddance," he said.

A long quiet. A really long quiet.

Then Jupiter looked at him. "My daddy is asleep," she said.

"Let's go back," I said.

"My daddy is asleep there?" she asked.

"Yes," I said.

When we got to the Far Pasture, Jupiter wanted to go into the pine woods.

"Not today," I said.

"Yes today."

"I know we always go there, but not today."

Jupiter took hold of both my ears and turned me.

"Today," she said.

So we went into the pine woods, where it was a little colder, and we wandered through the trees and I bent down so Jupiter wouldn't scrape her head against the branches. Mr. and Mrs. Joyce walked behind us, and after a few minutes Jupiter turned and held her hands out to Mr. Joyce, and he came up behind me and took her and settled her behind his head.

"Doesn't she look just like Madeleine at that

age?" said Mrs. Joyce.

Jupiter took Mr. Joyce's ears to steer him.

"Stop that," he said.

Jupiter did, but we only went a little farther before she said "Jackie" and reached down for me, and I reached up for her.

"I've got her," Mr. Joyce said.

"Jackie," said Jupiter.

"I said, I've got you," said Mr. Joyce.

"No, you don't," I said—and I may have said it too loudly, but I didn't care, because he knew exactly what I meant. I wanted him to know exactly what I meant.

I took Jupiter from his back and we walked home.

Mrs. Stroud was waiting in the yard.

"Did you have a good walk, precious?" she said.

"Jackie is mad," said Jupiter.

"I'm sure Jackie isn't mad," said Mrs. Stroud.

Jupiter shook her head. "Jackie is mad."

We went into the house together, and after I got her green boots off, she grabbed the stupid polar bear and I carried her upstairs to her room for her nap. She was already yawning.

"Jackie goonie-pie, are you going to stay while I fall asleep?"

I sat down in the rocker.

"Of course, Jupiter goonie-pie," I said, and she smiled, yawned again.

"I am not a goonie-pie."

"You are so a goonie-pie," I said.

She closed her eyes. "Am not," and she was breathing heavy in something like ten seconds.

I might have been breathing heavy too.

JUST BEFORE SUPPER that night, when the sun was low, Jupiter and I went out to the Small Barn again. The rope swing hangs down thirty-five feet from the top rafter, and the seat is so small that I can't use it anymore. But Jupiter can, and I pushed her again and again out of the barn's cool shadows, past the wide open barn doors, and into the golden light in the yard outside, so bright

I couldn't even see her when she began to swing back. Again and again she flew out of my life, and then came flinging back into it, until finally we'd had enough, and I caught her and held on to her tight.

THE NEXT DAY, Jay Perkins stopped by the house. It was a cold Sunday, and he was wearing his pink stocking cap.

"You want to run the loop?" he said.

Then Jupiter banged through the storm door and came down the stairs into the yard. "Jay goonie-pie!" she said.

He picked her up and she took off his stocking cap and dropped it on the ground.

"Hey!" said Jay Perkins.

She took hold of his ears.

"Jackie was mad," she said.

"What was Jackie mad about?"

"Everything," she said.

70

"That's a lot to be mad about."

"Are you going running?"

"When your brother gets his stuff on."

I went upstairs and got my stuff on. I found my bright yellow stocking cap on the stupid polar bear, took it off, and went downstairs.

"That's Solar's hat," said Jupiter.

"Solar?" said Jay Perkins.

"Solar the Polar Bear," I said.

Jay Perkins nodded and looked at Jupiter. "Is it okay if your brother wears it for when we run?"

Jupiter thought about that. "He can't get it all icky," she said.

"I'll try not to," I said, and we headed out.

We stretched by the end of our road. "You know," I said, "it is Sunday."

"So?" said Jay Perkins.

"We usually don't run on the weekends."

"I do," said Jay Perkins. "You know why?"

"Why?"

"Because I'm not going to be on varsity if I

don't run every day. You either."

"Thanks, Coach."

"I mean it."

"I know."

"So what were you mad about yesterday?"

"Nothing."

He looked at me. "Is that a lie?"

"Maybe," I said.

He shrugged. "It doesn't matter. I already know, anyway."

I looked at him.

"Everybody knows," he said.

"Everybody knows what?"

Jay Perkins reached down and tied his shoes. "About Jupiter. About her grandparents. About Canton's sister. About the legal fund Canton is putting together."

"The fund?"

"God, Hurd. You're not going to be on varsity someday if you're too stupid to figure out what it means to be part of a team."

"A team?"

72

"See?"

"Is that what you came to tell me today? That I'm supposed to be part of a team?"

"From now on, weekends too. And wear a decent sweatshirt, okay? No one gives a damn that you've been to Disney World."

MONDAY MORNING, I stopped by the gym. Coach Swieteck was in his office, gathering basketballs into his lap—which wasn't easy because his office was so small and there wasn't a whole lot of room to turn his wheelchair around. "There's a ball between the desk and the wall," he said. I leaned down, pulled it out, dropped it and looked around for a towel, found one and rubbed the ball down, then handed the basketball to him.

He watched me the whole time.

"Hurd, what was that all about?"

"It had a spider on it."

"A spider."

"I hate spiders," I said.

"Huh," he said. He pointed to a poster over his desk. "You know who that is?"

I didn't.

"He's the greatest runner of all time. Jesse Owens. You ever hear that name?"

"No."

"You have a two-page report on him due to me on Wednesday morning."

"Wait. Wait. You teach PE. I don't write papers for—"

"Three pages. Focus on what he did in the 1936 Olympics."

"Why am I doing this?"

"Because you are at this school for an education, and everyone should know who Jesse Owens is, and besides, you just killed my pet spider, you jerk. Bring those balls in the corner with you."

We went out together and Coach Swieteck began shooting baskets. He made most of them, which is impressive, considering he was shooting from a wheelchair.

"That's pretty good, Coach."

"Thanks so much, Hurd. I've been waiting all morning, just hoping for your approval."

"Jay Perkins stopped by yesterday."

"He probably wanted to check on your running."

"That's what he said. We're going to start running every day now."

"Good."

"I was wondering if you sent him."

"Why would you wonder that?"

"Because that's the kind of thing you do, Coach."

He took another two shots. Both swishes.

"Hurd, you have no idea what kind of thing I do," he said.

I went under the basket and caught three more swishes in a row and threw them back to him.

"Thanks, Coach."

"Don't you have Language Arts now?"

"Music."

"Go sing your heart out. And throw me those two balls by the bleachers on your way. And Hurd—"

"Yeah."

"Three pages by Wednesday."

I wrote four. Jesse Owens turned out to be worth it.

six

A COUPLE of weeks into May, spring started to get serious about its business. Suddenly those warm, yellow days followed one after another—the kind of days that Quintus Sertorius had loved, when the pines shrugged into brighter greens, and the red rhubarb really pushed out its stalks, and my mother collected all the house-plants and put them out on the south porch, and we yanked open windows closed since September.

Jupiter loved all the growing and the warming and the new smells and the sudden fresh green-gold leaves. She picked all the yellow forsythia blooms in one swoop and brought them in to my mother, who put them into a glass bowl on the kitchen table. Then she picked all the daffodils before they had bloomed, and my mother put those in a mason jar above the sink. Then my mother took Jupiter to where the tulip bulbs had sprouted and told Jupiter not to pick those.

I wasn't sure Jupiter understood.

On Saturdays my parents drove to Augusta— and sometimes after I got back from school. On those days, Jupiter and I would meet Jay Perkins at the end of our road and wave, and he'd stop and pick up Jupiter and she'd pull off his pink stocking cap and grab his ears and turn his head this way, that way, and they'd rub noses. He'd nod at me and head out while I took Jupiter from him and we walked back to the house.

On those days, I'd run by myself after my

parents got back. Sometimes at dusk. Sometimes in the dark.

It was on one of those afternoons, when my parents were over to Augusta and Jay Perkins had gone by and we'd waved, that Jupiter cut her legs up.

It all happened in a second. In less than a second.

Jupiter wanted me to push her on the rope swing.

I told her I'd be right there.

I went inside the Big Barn to check on the water for Rosie and Dahlia and Marcus Aurelius—we'd been having trouble with the pump—and Jupiter went into the Small Barn.

The pump was doing fine. I stopped to scratch Rosie on the rump.

And Jupiter opened the door to the storeroom in the Small Barn, and she went inside to explore. I figured later that she stepped into a loose ring of barbed wire we'd taken in last fall, and like that, it looped around her. It looped around her like a snake. She must have panicked, and immediately it tightened and grabbed at her and ripped at the soft chub of her legs and she started to scream.

When she saw me at the storeroom door, she reached out and fell and the barbed wire dragged itself over her and bit.

I held her with one hand and pulled the wire with the other, but the loops climbed up her legs and she screamed and cried and I carried her out into the light and the wire dragged behind her. She screamed again and I pulled the wire off her feet and ankles and most of the rest scraped down except some got caught behind her knee and bit again. And I was crying too now, but I pulled the barbs off and cupped them in my hand and lowered the wire until it was off her and I shook the barbs out of my palms and grabbed shrieking Jupiter and ran down our road.

I don't know who I thought I was going to find.

I found Jay Perkins, who had decided he'd run one more loop, who saw us and ripped off his shirt and wrapped it around Jupiter's legs, and we ran back to the house and he saw my father's pickup and told me to get the keys, and I handed Jupiter to him and found the keys hanging by the back door and I ran back out and I took Jupiter and Jay Perkins took the keys and we got into the cab.

"You know how to drive?" I said.

"Some," he said, and started the pickup.

He didn't hit anything until we got to the Sumner Medical Center.

And that was only because they put the stupid streetlight in the middle of the med center's parking lot.

Jay Perkins got out first, and then I scooted out the driver's side too because, you know, the stupid streetlight. I was still holding Jupiter, who was crying a little and holding me tightly but not shrieking—that's how brave she is—and we ran across the parking lot and into Emergency and the attending nurse at Triage stood up and in, like, three seconds there were four nurses and then another nurse with a wheelchair and I set Jupiter in it and they started to wheel her through a set of double doors.

"You'll have to wait here and give us some information," said the attending nurse.

Jupiter held out her arms. "Jackie!" she said. Not quietly.

"I'm going with Jupiter first," I said.

"I'm afraid—"

"I'll give you the information," said Jay Perkins.

"What relation are you to Jupiter?"

"I'm her brother," I said.

"I'm her cousin," Jay Perkins lied.

The nurse looked at us. "Cousin, you sit down and I'll send someone to find you a shirt. Brother, you go," she said, and she waved me away.

I gave my hand to Jupiter, and she grabbed it with both of hers, and we went into the examining room.

The barbed wire had bitten all over her legs, and sometimes they were more rips than bites. Jupiter held on to me with both hands while they wiped her legs down, and she started to cry again when the doctor came in and told her she was going to have a look at her legs now and was that all right?

"Jupiter, Jupiter," I said, "I'm right here. I'm right here. Look at me, okay? Just look at me. Keep looking right at my eyes. I'm right here. I'm always right here."

And you know what? She did. She kept looking right at my eyes. Even when a swab stung, or a bandage tightened, or when they gave her a shot so they could put in three stitches behind her left knee, she kept looking right at my eyes. And when Jay Perkins came in—and I didn't say anything about the white T-shirt he was now wearing that had a huge Mickey Mouse welcoming anyone who looked at him to the Magic Kingdom—when he came in, he stroked her hair and told her how brave she was and how he once had stitches and he cried a whole lot more than she did and she said "Really?" and he said "Yes, I did. A whole lot more."

And when the doctor finished, she said, "Jupiter, may I tell you a secret?"

Jupiter nodded.

"You are the bravest kiddo I have ever met."

And Jupiter smiled, and lay back on the bed, and closed her eyes. Even as she fell asleep, she was still smiling—which was a good thing, because that's the first thing my parents saw when they found us in the med center: Jupiter, asleep, with a smile.

They went right to the bed, and my father leaned down and kissed Jupiter on the forehead and my mother took her hand, gently so she wouldn't wake her up. They watched her for a long time, and then my father turned to me.

"You did well," he said.

"I shouldn't have left her alone. It was only for a second, and she—"

My father held up his hand. "Jack," he said, "there was an accident and you got her the help she needed. You got her here. By the way, how did you get her here?"

I should tell you, it's a good thing my father doesn't set a whole lot of store in cars and pick-ups, like some people who go bonkers if they get a stupid scratch on a bumper or something. I mean, it's just a pickup—and that day, it had done exactly what we needed it to do. The rest, my father said, didn't matter a damn.

THE DOCTOR AT the Sumner Medical Center told us that it might be wise to keep Jupiter overnight—just for one night. There were so many cuts and it would be easy for one to get infected. Having a nurse change all the dressings in the evening, and then again in the morning, might be the safest thing to do. So my mother drove Jay Perkins to his house and then drove home and gathered up some of Jupiter's clothes and all of her Elephant & Piggie books and Affy-Giraffey while my father went down to the hospital lobby and bought her a box of crayons and two animal coloring books. Even though Jupiter was sleepy, she took out all the crayons and spread them over her blanket, and then she colored every page of the first animal coloring book——she hadn't really gotten the concept of coloring inside the lines yet——and she got halfway through the second animal coloring book and had broken the point off of every crayon except for aquamarine before she lay back against her pillow, closed her eyes, and fell asleep again.

After that, she was mostly asleep, even after my mother came back with Elephant & Piggie.

The three of us sat beside the bed, not talking, not moving, and watched her.

Just watched her.

We watched her breathe slowly and quietly, in and out.

We watched her hold up her hands, and open them and close them.

We watched her eyes move beneath her eyelids, as if she were following Marcus Aurelius running through the Far Pasture.

We watched her turn her sweet face into the pillow, and open her lips as if to take a drink, and shake her head as if to say that she was *too* going to go into the pine woods. She was too. She was too.

If Joseph could have seen this miracle. His daughter.

If Joseph could have.

THERE WAS A day—it feels like a million years ago now—but there was a day when Joseph got a picture of baby Jupiter from her foster mother. He couldn't stop looking at it. He looked at it in the car all the way home from Brunswick to East Sumner. He kept it in his shirt pocket while we ate at a diner that night, and he would put his hand up to his heart to feel its edges, as if to be sure it was still there—the picture, but maybe his heart too. That night was wicked cold, and when we got home there wasn't much heat in our room. But Joseph stood by the window while I lay under two quilts in my lower bunk, and by the light of the moon and the stars, he stood there in only his boxers, the room so cold I could see his breath, and he held the picture of Jupiter in his hand and stared at it.

Then he came over to my bunk and sat down on it—I think the only time he ever did that. I guess he knew I was awake.

He held the picture out to me, but I couldn't see it in the dark.

"This is my daughter," he whispered, and he said it as if it were a wonder too great to be believed or understood. "My daughter," he said again. His whole body trembled in the warmth of the miracle.

I didn't have to say anything. He didn't want me to say anything. He just needed to speak the words out loud, as if speaking them would help him to understand, in the pale light that came out of the sky, that it was real.

That Jupiter was real.

That he was a father.

He went back to the window and looked outside, while I pulled the quilts over myself.

But then he said, "Look out the window, Jackie. Quick. Look."

I got up and stood beside him.

And maybe you're not going to believe this, but here's what happened next. The planet Jupiter swung in its orbit and framed itself in our window—which the frost was already starting to etch. Between the lines, Jupiter's light passed through and came across the dark of the room and lit it all up—almost like a full moon—and the light touched everything, as if it were trying to learn and know and understand, and it lingered on the shirt and sweater Joseph had left on the floor, on his backpack, on the library books he was reading, on the trig problem he'd left on his desk, on the brush on his dresser and the chair where he tied his shoes and the spot where he'd stand by the window, and Joseph said, as quiet and holy as if he were in a pew in First Congregational, "Damn."

He cupped his hands and lowered them into the light.

I think he was crying, but I wasn't sure.

Anyway, that's what happened.

I don't know if he ever went to bed, or if he stood in his boxers that whole night.

THE NEXT AFTERNOON, Jay Perkins was at the house a little bit early. He was wearing the Mickey Mouse T-shirt.

"How's Jupiter?" he said.

"Good," I said. "She's asleep upstairs."

"Nothing got infected?"

"Nope," I said.

"Good," he said. "You ready?"

"I thought I'd go back and get my Disney World sweatshirt."

"Shut up," said Jay Perkins, and we set off for three loops.

It was perfect. Sumner Hill Road was all bright green with the spring birches and Jefferson Hill was all red and gold with the spring maples. In Jenny's Notch, the rhododendrons in the sunny patches were already swelling with buds, and it felt and smelled like everything was just beginning, the way it does in springtime, with these sudden patches of forsythia and then groups of daffodils coming up through tall dead grasses and the ferns with the slick green they show and that good smell of earth and the smell that granite takes on when it's hot in the sun.

It was perfect.

Until the third loop, when we got to Mill Road, where Nick Porter and Brian Boss were waiting for us in Porter's pickup, which he could drive even as a sophomore on account of his farmer's license.

They pulled out behind us when we passed, and slowly followed—like some stupid animal that thought it was being so funny.

So stupid funny.

"Ignore it," said Jay Perkins, but it's hard to ignore a pickup that's prowling behind you on Mill Road, inching up close, then backing off, then with a grunt inching up close again, then backing off.

So stupid funny.

Jay Perkins never looked back. But I did. And every time I did, Nick Porter would jerk the pickup forward, like this time he really was going to run up our heels. And I could hear Nick Porter and Brian Boss laughing their stupid heads off.

They followed us all the way on Mill Road and turned up Sumner Hill Road when we turned.

And that's when Jay Perkins stopped. He leaned over the stone wall that runs along Sumner Hill Road, picked up a sharp rock the size of his hand, and turned toward the pickup.

Brian Boss, in the passenger seat and not all that far from the sharp rock and Jay Perkins, stopped laughing.

What you should know is that Jay Perkins, before he started running, was the pitcher for the East Sumner Wolverines, who went to State mostly because of Jay Perkins's pitching.

"You don't want to do that," hollered Nick Porter.

"Yes, I do," said Jay Perkins. "You can't believe how bad I do."

Nick Porter looked at me. "You did this," he said. "You broke up a team."

"It was never a team," said Jay Perkins. "It was just me and you two, like zits on my ass." He pulled his arm back a little more. "You like to drive with a windshield?"

"Let's get out of here," said Brian Boss.

Nick Porter looked at Jay Perkins. "Don't think this is over," he said.

"This is over," said Jay Perkins.

Nick Porter smiled. "Not your call, Mickey Mouse," and he started laughing again, and then he jerked the pickup past us and it spurted exhaust, gunning up Sumner Hill Road.

"We're behind time," said Jay Perkins, tossing the rock back onto the stone wall. "We're sprinting the rest of the way."

And we did.

Well, *he* did. I mostly did.

Then I threw up.

seven

MY father and mother made more trips to Augusta, and Miss Canton came out to the farm twice to meet with them and to walk around. She wanted to see Jupiter's surroundings, she said, and my mother took her through the house, and I took her through the Big Barn and the Small Barn and up to the Far Pasture. She asked to go to the family graveyard, and I took her there too, and showed her where the family slept, and Joseph's stone.

"This is still hard for you, isn't it, Jack?" she said.

I nodded.

"You must have loved him."

Nodded again.

"Why so much?"

"He had my back," I said.

Then *she* nodded.

"You know, Jack, this is going to be a fight."

"I know."

"And we may not—"

"Don't tell me that," I said.

"Okay," she said. "You know, I can see why my brother thinks so highly of you."

I looked at her.

"Mr. Canton and I sort of hate each other," I said.

She laughed. "Everyone thinks that Mr. Canton sort of hates them," she said.

"That's right," I said.

"They're wrong," she said.

"He hated Joseph," I said.

"There you're *really* wrong," she said. She ran her hand over Joseph's stone. "Let's get back."

"Wait a minute," I said. "What's that supposed to mean?"

She smiled. "If I had a dime for all the times my brother said the name Joseph Brook, I could give up lawyering. He had Joseph's whole career planned out for him."

"Really?"

"Really. He wanted Joseph to become a school principal."

I shook my head. "That would never have happened."

"Stranger things have happened. He thought Joseph was born for the job."

"He did?"

She looked at me. "Would I lie to you?"

"Maybe, because that sounds like a big one."

"Jack," she said, "who is more prepared to be a principal than someone who has fought with principals all his life?"

That did sort of make sense.

"So," I said, "does Mr. Canton have my career planned out too?"

"Yup," she said. "No lie."

You'd have been surprised too. I mean, Mr. Canton? My career?

I waited. Then I said, "What is it?"

She smiled. "Jack, I'm a lawyer. I work pretty hard at keeping confidentiality. Now, let's get back."

THE JOYCES CAME to visit again on a warm Saturday morning in May when all the purple lilacs were out and the bumblebees were hefting themselves to the blossoms and everything was smelling clear and bright like spring was finally here.

Jupiter and I were together in the rhubarb garden, turning over the rows between the plants and spreading some dried manure around the stems. Jupiter was getting bored, because we have a lot of rhubarb and it takes a while to turn over the rows, and because manure, even after a long winter drying, still smells like manure. And the thing is, none of us really like rhubarb. When it's cooking, my father says it makes the kitchen smell like—well, I won't tell you that. But it's easy to grow, and the deer won't eat the leaves, so every June my mother ruins perfectly good strawberries and makes strawberry-rhubarb jam and she brings it to the East Sumner Farmers' Market and sells it to people who I guess go home and eat it but I don't know why.

So we were out in the rhubarb garden and they drove up and Mrs. Joyce got out, and she called, "Jupiter sweetie, Grandmother's here," like she was making this big wonderful announcement, and it kind of broke my heart that Jupiter dropped the huge rhubarb leaf she was ripping into strips and ran straight across the rows and into Mrs. Joyce's arms, which Mrs. Joyce wrapped around Jupiter like she owned her.

Probably she thought she did.

Mr. Joyce got out too. He was smoking a

cigarette, for crying out loud.

I walked up to them, trying to wipe you-know-what off my hands. "Hi," I said.

They didn't say anything. I guess they knew I was the enemy.

My mother came out and down the porch steps.

"Hello," she said.

They said hello back. They probably knew she was the enemy too, but they had to say hello to her.

"We ask that folks don't smoke around here," she said. "It's a very old house and barn, and with all the hay lying around—you understand."

"I'll be careful," said Mr. Joyce.

My mother waited.

Mr. Joyce looked away and puffed.

"I really do have to insist," said my mother.

Mr. Joyce looked back at her, then threw the cigarette onto the grass and ground at it with his foot.

What a jerk.

"You're adopted, aren't you?" he said to me

suddenly—without looking up.

"I guess so," I said. "How do you know?"

"Part of the disclosure," he said. "So, do you ever wonder who your parents are?"

"I know who my parents are."

"Don't be cute," he said. "I mean, your biological parents. Your real parents."

"I know who my real parents are," I said.

"Okay," he said.

"Okay," I said.

Really. What a jerk.

"We thought we'd take Jupiter for a ride," said Mrs. Joyce. "She probably doesn't get off this farm much."

"You'll need a car seat," said my mother.

"Oh, don't worry. We're all set for our little sweetie."

"And you'll need to be back within—"

"We're aware of the conditions," said Mr. Joyce. He took out another cigarette and pushed it between his teeth, unlit.

"Within an hour," said my mother. "And don't

smoke when she's in the car with you."

Mr. Joyce didn't even look at my mother. "Let's get going," he said to Mrs. Joyce.

She picked Jupiter up, and Mr. Joyce opened the back door. They did have a car seat there, and piled next to it were a whole lot of toy animals that were brighter and fuzzier and floppier and cleaner than Affy-Giraffey had been in a long time. I could hear Jupiter squealing as she reached for them.

"Let me strap you in, sweetie," said Mrs. Joyce, and Mr. Joyce got in and started the engine while she fussed at the straps. Probably she hadn't done this in a long time, and probably Jupiter wasn't making it any easier, since she was reaching for the brighter fuzzier floppier cleaner toys. So finally Mrs. Joyce backed out and looked at me. "Young man, can you——"

I reached in and Jupiter dropped a striped camel and grabbed onto my ears. "Jackie goonie-pie," she said, "I love you."

"I love you too, Jupiter goonie-pie."

"I am not a goonie-pie," she said.

I clicked the straps together. "I'll see you in a

little while," I said.

"Are you coming?"

"No," I said.

"Why not?"

"They want you for themselves," I said.

"For how long?"

"Half a Saturday chore time," I said.

Jupiter thought about that.

"Okay, Jackie," she finally said. "Half a Saturday chore time."

I backed out and closed the door, and Mrs. Joyce went around the car and got in beside Jupiter. She handed her the striped camel, but Jupiter was watching me through the window, and waving, and dang, I was about to . . . you know.

"Bye-bye, Jackie goonie-pie!" she hollered.

They drove down the driveway.

"Bye-bye, Jupiter goonie-pie," I whispered.

My mother walked over and stood beside me. Her arm came up around my back, then onto my shoulders.

"You're going to be taller than I am soon," she said.

"I guess," I said.

I watched them drive down our road.

"You know, Jack, I don't tell you often enough how proud I am that you are our son." She pulled me close to her. "Or how much we love you."

Jupiter was out of sight. I didn't know where she was now.

"They'll be back soon," she said.

"Mom," I said, "if Joseph hadn't drowned, would he—"

"Yes," she said. "You'd have a brother." She took a deep breath. "And I'll be damned if we lose Jupiter too."

We both laughed, then—"You do realize you just cursed," I said.

"Really?"

I nodded.

"There are worse things in life, I suppose," she said, and she turned and went up the porch steps.

"But," she called, "he deserves it. What a horrible person he is!"

In her lifetime, I'm pretty sure that's the worst thing she had ever said about a human being.

Then she went inside, and I looked at our empty road, and went back to the rhubarb garden and the manure.

THE JOYCES WERE late coming back.

Really late.

It was midafternoon by the time they drove up, and when I opened the car door, Jupiter was dead asleep in the back seat—and not strapped into her car seat. Her face was painted like a cat and she was wearing some sort of stupid fairy costume. Her hand clutched a sparkling wand.

I reached in and lifted her out. She didn't wake up.

"I'm sorry we're so late," said Mrs. Joyce, "but the time absolutely flew by. We went to a small park and there was a carnival that had rides and music and face painting and little boutiques. Everyone we met loved Jupiter!"

My mother held her arms out and took Jupiter. "You're very late," she said.

"I know. I'm so sorry. Let me help you take her inside."

She followed my mother and Jupiter up the porch and into the house.

I stood with the horrible person.

He took out a cigarette, lit it, and threw the match down onto the ground.

"I'll never be able to kick these damned things," he said. He took a long pull of the cigarette. "You know, Johnny, I can help you find your real parents. I know who to connect you with."

"Jack," I said, and, "What's it to you?"

Another long pull off his cigarette. "Look, we can be civil about all of this. I'm offering to help you. We don't have to be enemies."

"You're trying to take my sister away from us. So yes, we do have to be enemies."

"And you're trying to keep my granddaughter

away from me. Did you ever think of it that way?"

"No. I didn't. Not once in all the months that you've ignored her."

Another long pull. Then with his cigarette, he gestured toward the house.

"She needs her. She's her grandmother."

"Then come visit her. That's what grandparents do."

He shook his head. "It's different."

"How?"

"I don't have to explain it to you, kid, so don't presume. You're not going to win. The day is coming when we're going to drive into all this mud"—he waved his arm across the farm—"and Jupiter will be coming home with us. Get used to the idea. There's nothing you or your little lawyer can do about it. Jupiter is my granddaughter, and we're going to take her, and she's going to grow up with us—like Madeleine should have."

"Joseph is my brother, and that makes Jupiter my niece, and she's going to grow up here, where she belongs, like Joseph should have."

He smiled and shook his head. "Not even a good try, Johnny—and Joseph, by the way, should have grown up in a prison, where he belonged." He took another long pull and blew out the smoke. "You should ask Jay about us," he said. "He'll tell you to give up before you get in over your heads."

"Jay? Jay Perkins?"

"He's got some sense. Talk to him," and Mr. Joyce threw the cigarette onto the drive, turned, got into the car, and honked the horn. I stepped on the glowing cigarette. Mrs. Joyce came running.

MONDAY MORNING WAS drizzly, the kind of rain that hovers in the air and gets blown back and forth with the wind's gusts. The lobby of East Sumner Middle was filled with dripping kids who were shaking off the drizzle, and Mr. Canton was in the middle of it all, directing like a traffic cop, pointing down the seventh-grade hall, then the eighth, then the sixth-grade hall, then back to the seventh to get kids to their lockers.

I went up to him.

"I'm kind of busy here, Hurd," he said.

"I heard something about you," I said.

"You're in middle school. I'm the vice principal. I bet you hear a lot of things about me."

"I heard that you thought Joseph Brook could
have grown up to be a principal in a school."

"Where did you hear that?"

"Your sister."

"For a lawyer, my sister can have a big mouth."

I waited.

"So what do you want me to say?" said Mr.
Canton.

I shrugged. "Nothing," I said. "Nothing. I
guess—I just wish that—that Joseph—"

Mr. Canton stopped directing traffic.

He looked down at me.

He put his hand on my shoulder.

You know how like in a movie, sometimes
everything suddenly stops, and the camera is on
just the characters you're supposed to be watching, and they're standing still in the middle of a

crowd, but they don't even see the crowd, because to them, nothing else matters in that moment?

You know how that looks?

That's how it was.

Mr. Canton said, "Me too," with his hand on my shoulder. And for a while everything held still . . . and then everything started up again, and Mr. Canton nudged me toward the eighth-grade hall. "You have first period in four minutes," he said.

I walked into the eighth-grade hall, but before I got to my locker, I almost stopped. What did he think I'd grow up to be? I really wanted to know.

But when I turned, Mr. Canton was the traffic cop again, and even though maybe something had changed between us, at least a little, I didn't go back.

Still, for the whole time I was in Music, while Ms. Uchida was directing us in "A Medley of John Lennon Songs," I really wanted to know.

eight

THAT afternoon, as soon as I got home, I changed into my running stuff, stretched in front of the house while Jupiter watched— "Funny Jackie goonie-pie!"—sprinted down our road to Sumner Hill, ran to Barlow Road, and turned. Barlow Road dips down to Barlow Pond, which maybe used to be a pond but is now more like a marsh, and in the springtime it's filled with early mosquitoes, so no one should run there. But

I did, and I got mosquitoes in my ears, in my eyes, in my mouth, until finally I circled back up and onto some granite ledges above the pond.

I know. I was being a jerk. But I just didn't want to run with Jay Perkins today. Not if he was friends with Mr. Joyce.

I kept up through the ledges, and then along Lower Gore Road, and when I turned on Sumner Hill Road again—and just so you know, even though this circle was shorter than the three loops I usually did, I'd lost a lot of blood—I looked ahead to see if Jay Perkins was around, but he wasn't.

I finished Sumner and took our turnoff in a sprint.

That's what I ran the next day, too.

And the next day.

But the day after that, Jay Perkins was waiting at the end of our road when I finished.

He was standing like he was mad, hands clasped up behind his head, not moving at all.

I ran to him and I leaned down with my hands on my knees.

"Where have you been?" he said.

"Running."

"Where?"

"Down to Barlow Pond."

"Then you're an idiot," he said. "This time of year, the mosquitoes—"

"I know," I said.

He turned around, then turned back.

"So what's going on?"

"What do you mean?"

"Cut it out, Hurd. Where have you been?"

"I told you. I ran down to—"

"Okay," he said, and he turned away again and started down Sumner Hill.

"How do you know the Joyces?" I called.

He stopped.

"Mr. Joyce said I should ask, so I'm asking. How do you know them?"

He didn't move.

"They're trying to take Jupiter away. Do you get it? They're trying to take— How do you know them?"

Jay Perkins turned around. He lifted the bottom of his Mickey Mouse shirt and wiped the sweat off his face. "They're my uncle and aunt," he said.

"What do you mean?"

"Do I need to explain it to you?"

"How come you never told me before?"

"Why should I?"

"*You* cut it out. You know why."

Jay Perkins walked back toward me.

"I don't need your drama, Hurd. I really don't. And if you don't want to run together, I don't care. You understand *that*? I don't care. *You* tell Coach that—"

"So that day in the med center, when you said you were Jupiter's cousin, you weren't lying?"

"Madeleine was my cousin."

"What?"

"Madeleine was my cousin."

"Again, why didn't you tell me?"

Jay Perkins looked like he was about to lay me out.

"What the hell, Hurd, why do you think?"

I really didn't know.

Jay Perkins stepped even closer, and remember, he was a lot taller than me, and maybe I'd slammed him into gym lockers once, but it was true that that happened when his back was turned to me—and it wasn't now.

"If it wasn't for Joseph Brook, Madeleine would be alive right now. Do you get *that*? She would be alive right now. And you didn't know her, and I get that it's not your fault. But Madeleine was the brightest spot in this whole crappy universe. She was the only thing that mattered in my lousy life. She was—"

And Jay Perkins started to cry.

Jay Perkins.

"She was the only one who . . ." he said.

And I thought, I really am a jerk. I should have known. I should have figured it out when he picked up Jupiter and kissed her the way he did.

"Not the only one," I said.

He shook his head. "The only one," he said.

"There's Jupiter."

It took a while, but Jay Perkins finally nod-ded, and then he and I walked together down the turnoff, and when we got past the tall pines and within sight of the house, there was Jupiter sitting on the steps with my mother, and she saw us, and she came running. First Jupiter hugged me around the knees, and then she hugged Jay Perkins around his knees. "Jay goonie-pie," she said, "missed you."

He picked her up and he kissed her on the fore-head the way he did, and when he went to put her down, she wouldn't let him. "Up, up," she said, and he put her on his shoulders and she grabbed both his ears and turned his head toward the house. "That way," she said—and he went.

She looked back. "Come on, Jackie goonie-pie!"

Jay Perkins looked back too. "What are you waiting for, Jackie goonie-pie?"

I followed them both, the sweat cooling on me as Jupiter steered Jay around the rhubarb garden, past the budding blackberries, around the house and under the high still-blossoming lilacs, up and down and up and down the front porch, through the Big Barn—where Jay had to lean down so Jupiter could scratch Rosie's rump—and outside again into the bright, bright sunlight that shone full on all three of us.

After Jupiter had gotten down—which was a while—and after she had kissed him and then me, and while Jay Perkins was stretching just a bit before heading off to finish his loops, I asked him what his uncle wanted him to tell me.

He shook his head.

"You don't want to know," he said.

"No, I really do," I said.

He stood up straight—he really was a lot taller than me. He looked into the house, where Jupiter was singing the eensy-weensy spider song, then back at me.

"He'd want me to tell you he always gets what he wants."

"Not always," I said. "He couldn't keep Joseph and Madeleine apart."

Jay Perkins nodded. "And now you know why this is such a big deal to him," he said. He stretched his back.

"One more thing," I said.

He waited.

"You need to help us."

Jay Perkins looked at me a long time.

"You need to help us," I said again.

"I don't need to do anything," he said.

"You don't want me to have to hurt you," I said.

He laughed and shook his head. "Let's do another loop, Hurd," he said. "You owe me."

A WEEK LATER, Coach Swieteck caught me in the hall. "What do you have next period, Hurd?" he said.

"Algebra."

"That's right," he said. "Come into my office." I followed him inside, and to his desk, where he wrote out a pass. "Take this to Mr. D'Ulney, then come back here. I got some stuff for you to do."

"Coach, I'm supposed to—oh, right—you're not interested."

He nodded. "Good to see you're making progress in your education. Get going."

When I got back, he did have some stuff for me to do, but none of it was all that big a deal. One of the bleachers had to be pulled against the wall, and it does take two to wind the cables together—and before we did it I had to climb under them to rescue some of the loose basketballs. And some new weights had come that had to be unpacked and loaded onto the Universal—and that took two people too. And there were some mats that had to be dragged outside and aired out, which you already know he could do himself, but it's easier with two people. Stuff like that.

Before the period was half over, after we'd taken out the last mat, we walked—I walked, he wheeled—back across the gym, and he said, "So, Perkins said he thinks you wanted to hurt him the other day."

I looked at him.

"I guess so," I said.

"Don't try. He's thin but he's tougher than he looks."

"So am I," I said.

Coach looked at me. "Not that way," he said. "You want to tell me what it was about?"

I shook my head.

He wheeled ahead of me a little, then turned. "You think I put you guys together because I figured you needed him, right?"

"It's pretty obvious, Coach."

He smiled and shook his head. "I'm a whole lot more subtle and complex than that, Hurd. And so are the two of you."

"What do you mean?"

"Go to class. You got twenty minutes to do what you have to do in Algebra—solve for x or y or whatever it is you do there. Thanks for helping me out. Now get going."

"Wait. What—"

"Nineteen minutes. You better hurry." And he wheeled away toward his office.

But I cut in front of him.

"That's not fair. You don't get to do that."

"Do what?"

"Just throw out some hint and then wheel away."

"I'm a teacher," he said. "That's like being a god. I can do whatever I want."

"Tell me," I said.

"Listen, Hurd, I'm not interested in—"

"Tell me."

He looked at me a long time. "Dang," he said finally, "you really are making progress in your education." He shook his head. "So, okay, Jay Perkins has had a pretty rough life. Maybe rougher than yours. But it's not my story to tell. Ask Perkins yourself. He'll tell you if he wants you to know. But I will say this: A good coach always knows who to team up. And I, Jackson Horatio Hurd, am a great coach."

"How did you know about 'Horatio'?"

He smiled. "Yeah, if I were you, I wouldn't let that get around. Talk to Perkins after you run today"—and he wheeled away.

So I did.

That afternoon, we finished our three loops and we were heading down the turnoff so Jay Perkins could say hi to Jupiter, and I said, "When are you going to tell me why your life is so lousy?"

"Wow," he said, "that is so not any of your business."

"Coach told me to ask."

"He would."

"Tell me about Madeleine," I said.

He stopped. He waited. I waited.

And then he told me. Like he had been waiting all this time to tell me.

How beautiful she was—long dark hair down to her waist, green eyes, perfect smile. How she was a runner too, and she hated that she could never beat him—and how he wished now he had let her once or twice. How she was smart. How she knew how to shut up and listen, like when he told her that—

Like when he told her that his father said—

His father said that when he and Jay's mother split up, they had a huge fight over who had to take him. Not who *got* to take him. Who *had* to take him.

He was six. He remembered every word.

How his father reminded him all the time that he *had* to take him.

How his father kept getting fired because all he knew how to do was complain and complain until his boss would get sick of him and tell him to get out. And then his father would complain and complain about his crummy boss and he'd keep on until he got the next boss.

How when he was ten his father started leaving him alone to go wherever. And how sometimes there wasn't food in the house.

How his uncle and aunt looked down on him and his father because they had nothing. But not

Madeleine. How his uncle and aunt had never even been in his house, and how they didn't want him in their house, but Madeleine invited him anyway. How his aunt told him he should get a paper route so he had enough to get a decent haircut. How she once left bars of soap by their front door with his name on the package. How none of them, his father or his uncle and aunt, had ever gone to see a single game he'd been in—but Madeleine came to them all, and she cheered whenever he did anything. She called him "Cousin" like it was a claim.

Like it was a claim.

How she had a huge fight with her father and how she made him take Jay out to breakfast and apologize for being a jerk to Jay, and how ever since, Jay and his uncle had breakfast together on Wednesday mornings.

How his uncle had turned out to be not the total hard-ass he had always seemed to be—even though it took Jay a long while to figure that out. How he had once promised Jay that he'd be on his side every time.

Every time.

Every single time.

"Perkins," I said quietly. "Perkins, I need you to be on my side now."

Long silence.

"Perkins, I need you to tell him to let Jupiter stay with us."

Jay Perkins shook his head. "He won't—"

"Jay, tell him Jupiter is happy. Tell him Jupiter will grow up on a farm that she loves. She will grow up with a family she loves, and who love her. Tell him we'll be at every one of her basketball games, and her science fairs, and her robotics club competitions, and her middle school musicals. Tell him—"

"Shut up, Hurd. I get it. Okay? I get it."

"Tell him that Madeleine would want her to stay with us."

Jay Perkins looked away to the three mountain ranges beyond the farm. It was a hazy day, so you couldn't see the peaks really, or how they all fit together. It was all mixed up in a sort of blue wash.

Then Jay Perkins turned back and pulled out a silver chain from under his shirt. "She gave me this," he said. "She gave it to me on my thirteenth birthday. It's the only thing I have that someone ever gave me. I threw away the stupid bars of soap."

"You did get the Mickey Mouse shirt from the Sumner Medical Center."

He laughed. "Yeah. I guess I did get that."

And that's when we saw Jupiter, who must have been tired of waiting, suddenly running down our road, hollering, "Jay goonie-pie! Jackie goonie-pie! Jay goonie-pie! Jackie goonie-pie!" and my father followed her, laughing and laughing. She hugged me around the knees and then she hugged Jay Perkins around the knees and he picked her up and set her on his shoulders and she, of course, grabbed his ears.

My father couldn't stop laughing as she pulled Jay Perkins around and around by the ears, and then she said, "Make pancakes with us, Jay goonie-pie!"

"I don't know, Jupiter. Maybe some—"

"Wednesday is pancakes-and-sausages night," said my father. "It's getting late, and we'd be glad to have you at our table. I could drive you home afterward—or, given your past experience with the pickup, you could drive and I'll ride shotgun."

And Jay Perkins said, "Okay. But you really have to let me drive."

"You know you don't have a license," my father said.

"Did you have a license when you started to drive?" said Jay Perkins.

My father smiled. "You have me there," he said. Then he looked at me. "Don't even ask."

You know what? Sometimes the universe works out right. It just does.

That night, Jay mixed up the batter, and Jupiter plunked in the frozen blueberries, and my father and mother tended the griddle, and I fried up the sausages and some bacon too, and then we sat down with hot maple syrup and cold milk, and I looked over at Jay and thought about how he and Joseph might have gotten to be friends if there had been time—if, instead of *sometimes*, the universe worked out right *all* the time.

Afterward, Jay Perkins and I got in the pickup with my father and Perkins drove home. He stopped at the end of his driveway, I think because he didn't want us to see the house. But there was still some light in the sky, and it being spring and most of the branches not leafed out all the way, we could see it through the trees.

My father didn't talk the whole way home.

nine

THE weekend before the hearing, Miss Canton came to the house and we sat around the kitchen table together while Jupiter was down for her two o'clock nap.

"The hearing is preliminary," she said. "The judge is hoping that the two parties can come to an agreement and there will be no need for a more formal procedure with witnesses."

"Witnesses?" said my mother.

"Legal experts, child psychologists, staff from the Sumner Medical Center. The Joyces have a great many resources, and it's likely we'll see them all on full display if we go beyond this hearing." She looked at me. "Even your adoption process will be up for scrutiny."

My mother took my father's hand.

"I have an idea," I said. "How about if the Joyces just get out of our lives? We can come to an agreement about that."

"Jack," said my mother.

"He's right," said my father.

"Bradley," said my mother.

"I don't think that's going to happen," said Miss Canton. "So let's walk through this. We'll meet first in the courtroom, then we'll be with the judge in her chambers—that's another way she hopes to keep this informal. Both couples will be there, of course, and all the attorneys."

My father leaned forward. "*All* the attorneys?"

"Me, and their three."

My father sat back.

"The judge will explain that the central issue here is the well-being of Jupiter Brook. Our side will take the position that your family has fostered Jupiter at the State's request, and since then has been following the adoption procedure for well over a year. You have undergone all the appropriate oversight. Jupiter is healthy and happy and well cared for. And the continuity provided by this loving family is critically important to the emotional health of a very young child. Their side will argue that they are Jupiter's biological grandparents, her closest living relatives with the possible exception of her paternal grandmother, whose whereabouts is unknown. They will argue that they have lost a daughter and endured terrible grief—which we have to acknowledge. And they will argue that they have the financial resources for supporting Jupiter in every way—which we also have to acknowledge."

"How about that they didn't want Jupiter after she was born?" I said. "How about that?"

Miss Canton nodded. "If things turn negative

in the preliminary hearing, that might come up. But they might counter that they were traumatized by their daughter's death and needed time to come to the right decision. They might also counter— and again, only if things turn negative—that the life you provide on a working farm is by its nature much more dangerous to a young child than the life they can provide. You have to know that they will bring up the barbed wire."

"That was an accident," my father said.

"Of course it was. I understand that," said Miss Canton. "But put that incident in the hands of three smart lawyers—an obvious danger, a minor attending, another minor driving without a license because the parents are absent—"

"But—"

Miss Canton raised her hand. "Bradley, I understand. I'm on your side. But I want you to hear how it will sound."

"Is there anything else?" said my mother.

Miss Canton turned to me. "I'd like you to be in court too," she said. "You can't be in chambers—at least, not at first. But I may ask the judge to meet you if things are going badly."

"Why?" said my father.

"Jack was your foster child when you adopted him," she said. "The parallels are obvious, and she might want to meet someone who grew up in your household under those circumstances."

"I can do that," I said.

"Would their lawyers ask him questions too?" my mother said.

Miss Canton shook her head. "I'd ask that the judge meet with him alone. But again, if we do move beyond the preliminary hearing, it may come to that."

My father released my mother's hand. He stood, walked around the kitchen, then leaned down on the back of his chair and looked at Miss Canton. "You need to be straight with us," he said.

"I always am."

"Good," he said. "So be straight now. Are we going to lose our daughter?"

My mother put her hand up to her face. Then

she reached over and held my hand.

Miss Canton took off her glasses and set them on the table. Dang, everything was so quiet. I could hear Marcus Aurelius stomping in his stall.

"Bradley," she said, "the Joyces are Jupiter's biological grandparents. Their daughter has died. It's more than possible that you will."

I left after that. In the Big Barn, I scratched Rosie's rump and put some new oats in Marcus Aurelius's bin. Out the back barn door, and to the Far Pasture, and then down the ledges to the graveyard. I sat by Joseph's stone. It was midafternoon now and the sun had gone pale. Cold air was coming in. I sat with my back against the stone. It was still warm.

I told Joseph what Miss Canton had said.

I asked him how he'd be if something happened and I wouldn't always know where Jupiter was.

It was hard to get it out, but that's what I asked.

I waited. There wasn't any answer.

Probably because I already knew the answer.

• • • • •

WHEN I GOT back to the house, Jupiter was up. We played Candy Land, which, when you're playing with a three-year-old kiddo, can take about five hours—except it got cut short by supper.

Then after supper, we played "animal dessert" with Affy-Giraffey and Solar the Polar Bear, which could also have taken five hours, except bedtime came in one.

At bedtime, we read every book she had about cows—and you'd be surprised at how many little kid books about cows there are.

And after the last cow book, my mother and father and I tucked Jupiter in, and we all kissed her good night, and my mother sang a song about a purple cow who likes purple grass and makes purple milk for purple people, and Jupiter went to sleep.

Then the three of us went downstairs and sat in front of the wood stove while my father made up the fire, and my mother brought out mugs of tea because it was going to be a cold night, she said, and we all three sat there, watching the new flames take hold, not drinking our tea, and trying not to hear Miss Canton's words that had been echoing in the house all this time: "It's more than possible that you will."

And so the week went by.

It wasn't on the highlights film of my middle school academic performance.

Mrs. Halloway reminded me that when she assigned *The Pearl*, she expected that all of her students would read *The Pearl*, including me, and she was aware that this was our second book by John Steinbeck, which, though she didn't feel she needed to justify her choice of novels for her classes, she had chosen in order to compare two great works by the same writer—and she didn't mind if I thought they were both depressing, except that since I hadn't even finished chapter one, saying that the book was both depressing and dumb didn't exactly carry a whole lot of weight with her.

Mr. Collum looked at my lab report on

inherited genes and suggested that Father Mendel would never have accepted this—and neither would he. "Do it again," he said. "This time, with some effort."

Mr. D'Ulney pointed out that there was a reason I needed to show all my work on my algebra problems, since the notion that I could just come up with the answer without being responsible to anyone for explaining *how* I came up with the answer was the provenance of Huns, barbarians, dictators, tyrants, and assorted fools—whom I did not want to grow up to be, right?

Ms. Uchida told me she was disappointed that I hadn't taken the time to memorize the line I had to sing for the John Lennon medley. "Jack," she said, "it's one line. You can't remember one line? Okay, here's a hint: it's about a submarine, and it's what color?"

"Gray," I said.

Aren't all submarines gray?

But I guess not, since she let out her breath slowly. "Only if you're color-blind," she finally said.

I think Coach Swieteck understood. He told me that if I wanted to skip the volleyball unit, I could run laps outside instead.

That was a pretty easy choice.

And I know Mr. Canton understood. Whenever he saw me in the halls, he looked at me like he knew what I was thinking. He didn't do some stupid thumbs-up thing, or say something like "It's going to be fine," or give me a pat on the back like everything was okay. He looked at me like he knew that sometimes the world could be pretty crappy, and he understood.

And somehow, the way he looked, I knew he expected me to understand that too.

That's what the week was like—that and trying to squeeze in every moment I could with Jupiter, and almost crying every time she called me "Jackie goonie-pie," and playing with her in the afternoon and reading to her at night, and then my parents and me sitting by the wood stove after she fell asleep, them pretending to read, me pretending to do algebra and fix my stupid inherited gene project, and no one talking because we were afraid of what we would say.

THE HEARING WAS on Friday. We drove over to Augusta with Jupiter in her car seat, talking about every single thing she saw along the way: the trees, the clouds, the McDonald's with a playground, the blue car, the red car, the other blue car, the black car, the other McDonald's with a playground, the other red car, the big white truck, the garbage truck, the yellow school bus, the yellow umbrella, the yellow light, the yellow-shirt man on the telephone pole, the purple lilacs like the ones next to the Small Barn, the other other red car, the other other McDonald's with a playground—

None of us told her to quiet down.

We parked near the statehouse and walked over to the courthouse. Miss Canton was waiting for us, and Jupiter ran into her arms. Miss Canton hugged her hard, then I took Jupiter's hand and we all walked inside.

There were a lot of marble steps to walk up.

Jupiter thought the steps were great.

Every step echoed.

Jupiter thought the echoes were great too—especially since "goonie-pie" came back pretty clearly when she yelled it out.

It was cold. "It's always cold in here," said Miss Canton.

Jupiter didn't care.

We went into a small office and gathered at a table. Jupiter sat on my lap and Miss Canton took a coloring book and a small box of crayons out of her briefcase and passed them over to us.

The blinds were shut and made the room dark. It was cold in here too.

"I think you know what to expect," said Miss Canton. "The Joyces are already seated in the courtroom. They're on the right side; you'll sit on the left. After a little while Judge Benedict will send someone to call all of you into her chambers. I'll come with you, and the Joyces will come with their lawyers. Jack, until then you'll need to stay out here in the waiting area with Jupiter. Can you do that?"

I nodded.

"Everyone, we all have to be calm and natural. I know it's hard. There is so much at stake. And the place itself is so . . . unnatural. But just be yourselves, answer any questions, don't let anything rile you—no matter what they say. Show them how much you love your daughter and how she has thrived with your care."

My parents both nodded. But you could tell that my father especially wanted to be anyplace in the world but here.

"All right," Miss Canton said. "Then let's go inside."

"One thing," I said.

They all three looked at me.

I could hardly get the words out.

I could hardly get the stupid words out.

"You've got to win," I said.

Miss Canton took a deep breath. "We'll do our best," she said. Then she opened the office door and we walked echoing toward the courtroom. Miss Canton opened the big doors and followed my parents inside. She looked back at me, and then the doors closed, and Jupiter and I sat down on a bench in the hall that someone needed to put a stupid cushion on, and we began to wait.

We waited a long time.

A very long time.

Jupiter finished the coloring book and wanted to color the bench too. She wasn't all that happy when I took her crayons away.

We watched people walk up and down the stairs for a while, and we imitated the way that some of them walked. This was fun until a guard saw us doing this too many times.

I told Jupiter the story of how Joseph went down to Brunswick to find her and how he found the house where she was and stood outside in the freezing cold. I told her how he got her baby picture and I showed it to her, since I still kept it in my wallet. "I was little then," she said.

We decided to walk outside and around the

courthouse, and Jupiter dragged me down the marble stairs, past the annoyed guard, and out into the bright sunshine—which looked nice and warm but a cold front had dropped onto Augusta and it was freezing—and I mean, freezing like you-could-see-your-breath freezing. We walked around the courthouse once, then marched around once, then skipped around once, and then I said, "Jupiter, let's go back inside," and so we did, and we went back to the bench without the cushion and I tried not to think about what was happening in the courtroom.

"Jackie crying?" said Jupiter.

"Just because of the cold," I said.

"Jackie, don't cry," she said.

I held her, and then I let her climb on my back, and we walked in front of the door to the court-room like an elephant, then like a piggie, then like a giraffe (which is hard), then like a polar bear, then like a seahorse (which is pretty hard too), and just when we were about to start walking like a monkey, the door opened and my parents came out, and Miss Canton came out behind them.

Jupiter reached for my mother, who took her and held her.

My father said, "Everything go . . . Did everything go okay out here?"

"Yes," I said. "Did everything go okay in there?"

No one said anything.

No one said any freaking thing.

"Okay," I said.

"Judge Benedict would like to speak with you, Jack," said Miss Canton.

I looked at my parents. My mother nodded.

"Okay," I said.

"She'll want to ask some questions about growing up with your family."

"Okay," I said.

"It'll be fine, Jack. Just be yourself."

"I guess," I said. "It's not like I have anyone else to be."

Miss Canton smiled. "No, you don't," she said. "Let's go."

My mother kissed me lightly, and my father

shook my hand—really, he shook my hand, which he'd never done before. I heard Jupiter ask, "Where Jackie going?" and then the courtroom doors closed behind me.

ten

I T was cold in here too.

We walked by rows of wooden seats like the pews in First Congregational, and then through a swinging door in the low wall at the front of the courtroom. The Joyces were sitting with their three lawyers, heads all close together, and they glanced up at me when I came through. Mr. Joyce looked away, but Mrs. Joyce smiled, as if that would make everything okay.

"We'll go this way," said Miss Canton, and she led me behind the judge's bench, through another door, and down a hall.

"Why is it so cold everywhere?" I said.

"It is cold," she said. "And it's worse because you're a little bit nervous. Everyone is."

"I guess," I said.

And then Miss Canton stopped, knocked at a door, and held it open.

"This is just you, Jack," she said, and I walked in.

The office was warm.

"Jackson Horatio Hurd," said Judge Benedict. "I'm glad to meet you." She came around from behind her desk and held out her hand.

I shook it. "Glad to meet you."

"Sit down here." She pointed to a chair by the bay window. "It's my favorite spot in the office. In the winter, the frost puts on this miraculous light show, and in the springtime, those maples are golden—they're just past that now."

"We have sugar maples on our land. Every

spring we tap them."

"How much syrup do you get?"

"Fifteen gallons—sometimes a little more."

"Did Jupiter help with that this year?"

"Some."

"I bet she helps you eat the syrup."

"She does. She loves it."

It wasn't what I expected at all. Not Judge Benedict. And not the office. Books on high shelves filled one whole wall, and they spilled onto the tops of wooden file cabinets whose drawers didn't quite close, they were that full. A bright, bright painting hung on one wall, filled with huge flowers whose colors looked like they could leak right out of the frame. Portraits hung on the other walls.

"Recognize any of those?" said the judge.

"Some," I said. "Emily Dickinson and Langston Hughes. We studied them both in Language Arts."

"Two of my favorite poets. I'm glad you studied them. Who else?"

"Henry David Thoreau."

"He could be obnoxious," she said, "but I like

his writing enough to keep him around. How about that one?"

"Jesse Owens."

"Jackson, I'm surprised you know Jesse Owens. You didn't study *him* in Language Arts."

"My PE teacher has his picture over his office desk. He'd give anything to run like Jesse Owens."

"So would everybody else."

"Not like my PE teacher would."

Judge Benedict nodded. "I think someday I'd like to visit your school. Do you know why I keep those pictures on my wall?"

I shook my head.

"All those people had a fierce belief that if anyone tried hard enough, they could figure out what was right and what was wrong—no matter how hard or knotty the problem. Do you think they were right?"

I waited a moment to think about what I was going to say—then just said it anyway. "I think if they were here, and they wanted you to do what is right, they'd tell you that Jupiter belongs with us."

She smiled and shook her head. "I wish it were that easy."

"It is that easy," I said. "She loves us, and we love her, and the Joyces are jerks."

Judge Benedict leaned down. "Think for a moment as a judge, Jackson."

"Really?"

"Just for a moment, think as a judge. Do you believe your opinion of the Joyces is unbiased?"

"What does that mean?"

"Is it possible that you think the Joyces are jerks because they want to take Jupiter away from you?"

"Of course."

Judge Benedict sat back a little bit and smiled. "That's an honest answer."

"So," I said, "think for a moment as Jupiter's brother—"

"Jackson, you're not technically—"

"No, I mean you. Think as her brother. Is it possible that even if some stupid law might say that the Joyces should get Jupiter, could it still be wrong to let them?"

Judge Benedict thought about that a long time. "I suppose that's possible," she said. "Sometimes a law cannot take into account all the circumstances around a certain case."

"That's an honest answer too," I said.

Judge Benedict smiled again. "That's what judges try to do," she said. "Speaking of which, Miss Canton tells me that her brother is your vice principal."

"That's right," I said.

"Apparently he has your whole life planned out."

"I guess—except he won't tell me the plan."

"Telling it would ruin it," she said. "And probably he wants you to find out for yourself. And you will, you know."

"I guess," I said again. "Right now I'm making plans to secretly take someone across the border into Canada where we will never be found."

She went back behind her desk. "And that is

definitely not thinking like a judge."

"Maybe I can just hide her on the farm. I could, you know. There's a million places."

"Yeah, let's come back to terra firma. Jackson, I'd like to ask you something else. Something rather personal."

"Okay."

"What is your earliest memory, before you went to live with the Hurds?"

I thought about that for a while. "I'm sorry," I finally said. "I don't think I have any from before."

"What's your earliest memory, then?"

"That's easy. My mother is holding me on her lap. She smells like peppermint. It's Christmas Day and the tree is all lit, and there are presents, and she tries to put me down so I can go open them, but I won't get down."

"Really? You didn't want to go open the presents?"

"No."

"Why not?" Judge Benedict watched me. It

seemed like this was an important question to her. But the answer was easy too.

"Why should I? I already had everything I wanted."

She sat back in her chair.

"Jackson, do you think Jupiter already has—"

"Yes," I said. "She does."

"Did Joseph?"

"In the end he would have."

"Did Madeleine?"

"I don't know."

"Do the Joyces?"

A long time. "No," I finally said.

"And *that* answer," said Judge Benedict, "is thinking like a judge."

And when she said that, I knew two things.

First, I knew what Mr. Canton thought I was going to be—and I wasn't sure I wanted to be that. It might hurt too much.

But second, I knew we weren't going to get Jupiter.

W<small>E DIDN'T HEAR</small> from Judge Benedict over the weekend.

The cold stayed behind us in Augusta, and we came back to those first really warm days of early summer, when you're sweating after lifting just a couple of bales, and the hay is sticking to your arms and finding its way down the back of your T-shirt. Marcus Aurelius carried Jupiter and me down to the Far Pasture and up into the pine woods, and we played hide-and-seek—except you remember she didn't really know how to hide. Jupiter was the only one who talked at supper—which was fine by her—and every time the phone rang, we all felt sort of sick.

Jay Perkins didn't come by to run the whole weekend, so I did four loops on Saturday and four loops on Sunday by myself, pounding Sumner Hill Road like I could hurt it. It was warm enough that I didn't need to wear Jay Perkins's bright yellow stocking cap, but I wore it anyway.

On Monday morning, we still hadn't heard from Judge Benedict, and I almost asked to stay home and wait with my parents—but I didn't want to. I didn't want to be there when we heard.

You remember how I said East Sumner is tiny and everyone knows everyone else's business? And how even though everyone knows everyone else's business, no one talks about it—which makes things weird sometimes?

That's how it was when I got on the bus on Monday morning. I guess everyone knew we were waiting to hear about Jupiter, and so the bus driver watched me get on, and I could feel her eyes the whole time I walked down the aisle. But she didn't say anything.

Fine.

Everyone I didn't much know watched me too. Nothing from them.

Fine.

John Wall and Danny Nations and Ernie

Hupfer watched me as I walked to the back seat, where I used to sit with Joseph.

Fine.

Except before the bus got into gear, those three guys got up, came to the back of the bus, and sat around me. They didn't talk.

Okay. We go as far as we can go, I guess. You can't expect more.

When we got to school, I was the last one off the bus, and John and Danny and Ernie each punched me on the arm, and we headed to our lockers.

In the lobby, Mr. Canton was directing traffic as usual, waving kids to the halls they were supposed to go to. But when he saw me, he stopped. He looked at me with his hands still up in the air waving, like his hands knew all the moves and didn't have to pay attention.

He finally took them down out of the air and he walked toward me and without a word, Mr. Canton—this really happened—Mr. Canton bent over and put his arms around me. He didn't say anything. He put his arms around me.

He really did.

If a galactic spaceship had landed on the lawn outside school and crushed the flagpole—

And if sixteen alien creatures eight feet tall had come out and slimed their way across the burned lawn—

And if the sixteen alien creatures had stopped and joined together in "A Medley of John Lennon Songs" before climbing back into their galactic spaceship and heading to wherever home was—

I would have been less amazed than I was in Mr. Canton's arms.

Finally he let me go and took a step back. "Jack, you've been through a whole lot."

"We haven't heard yet," I said.

"I know," he said. "Maybe today?"

"Maybe," I said.

"Maybe good news."

I shrugged.

"Okay," he said. "Okay. Jack, I need you to go

down to the gym. Coach Swieteck is waiting for you."

"I've got homeroom."

"I've already taken care of that."

"Okay," I said. "Does he need—"

"Just head down there. And by the way, don't think I'm ever going to do that again."

"You mean the h—"

"Coach Swieteck is waiting."

I went down to the gym. I figured Coach would be shooting baskets or making some other eighth grader drag mats around, but he wasn't. It was quiet as tombs there, and I knocked at the office door, and Coach said, "Go away," and I called through the door that Mr. Canton told me to come down to the gym, and Coach opened the door, backed away, told me to come in and shut the door, and then he turned to his desk, which Jesse Owens was still running over.

"Hurd," he said, "I hate to tell you this, since enough has happened to you—is happening to you. But I think it has to be me."

"We haven't heard about Jupiter yet, Coach. And it's not—"

"Hurd," he said—and he started to choke up.

Really, he started to choke up.

"Coach?" I said.

"Shut up," he said, "and just let me say this. Okay? I don't think I can do it unless I get it all out at once, okay? So shut up."

"Okay," I said.

Then he told me what happened on Saturday. How Jay Perkins was running through Jenny's Notch. It was probably before dinnertime. He was on the east side of the road, right where it dips down to a steep drop into pines. Someone came up behind him, maybe in a pickup truck, probably pretty quickly, and whoever it was didn't even try to slow down since the truck didn't leave any tire marks. It hit him almost square.

"No, don't interrupt me, Hurd. Just don't interrupt me."

The impact shattered Jay Perkins's left leg and broke his hip. It threw him into the pines, which saved him from tumbling all the way down the slope into the Notch, but it broke five, maybe six ribs. It also snapped his head into one of the pine trunks. He was probably unconscious before he hit the ground and smacked his face against an out-cropping.

The driver—damn him—kept going.

Jay Perkins's father—damn him too—didn't come home until late. He figured that Jay had gone ahead and eaten something for supper, and he didn't bother to see if he was in his room upstairs. He went to bed around midnight and never checked. He didn't wake up until noon—at least, that's when Jay's father said he woke up. He never reported his son missing.

Jay was out in the pines all night long. In noth-ing but that stupid Mickey Mouse T-shirt he wears.

In the morning, Jay Perkins woke up. He could only open his right eye—the outcropping had bashed up the left side of his face. He couldn't move his left leg, of course. He couldn't move hardly anything at all. He tried calling for help, but it's not exactly like there's a whole lot of people strolling through Jenny's Notch on a Sunday morning. So he had to pull himself up along that incline—no one knows how he did it with a broken hip, but he did. He pulled himself up until he got even with the road. Then he fell unconscious again.

That was how Mr. D'Ulney found him. Mr. D'Ulney was the one who told Coach all this. He was heading back to school because he'd left some grading behind, and he decided to go through the Notch because it's a whole lot prettier than the highway, and he saw this broken kid in the gravel. If he hadn't forgotten his grading . . .

That's where Coach Swieteck stopped.

"Is he—"

He handed me a note. "Here's permission to leave the school grounds. Mr. Canton wrote it out already. He also called your parents, and he got someone to teach Ms. Uchida's music class. She's outside in the parking lot, waiting for you. Go."

I did.

The whole way there, we didn't talk, Ms. Uchida and me. It was like being on the bus again. But I mean, what was she supposed to say? "Jack, how are things going?" "Jack, here's someone else you care about who may die"? "Jack, you think maybe you'll lose your sister and Jay Perkins too?" "By the way, how are classes these days?"

What was she freaking supposed to say?

We arrived at the same hospital where we'd taken Jupiter. The same person who had asked Jay Perkins about Jupiter now asked what our relationship was to Jay Perkins.

"Teacher," said Ms. Uchida.

"Friend," I said.

"You'll have to wait," she said. "Right now they're only allowing family."

"I'm family," I said.

She looked at me.

"My sister is Jay Perkins's cousin's daughter."

She looked at me some more, like she couldn't quite figure that out.

"Please," I said.

"You'll still—"

"Please," I said again.

She shook her head—but she also smiled. She looked at her computer screen. "Room 115. Just a few minutes—even if you are the brother of your sister who is Jay Perkins's cousin's daughter— whatever that means."

"I'll wait here," said Ms. Uchida, and so I went to find my friend.

eleven

I COULD hardly breathe as I passed room after room.

Some of the them were empty—nothing but a bed and the blue-dark light. Some had people lying on high beds, not moving beneath still sheets, monitors rolled up beside them. The sick-sweet smell of chemicals. Nurses on thick-soled shoes walking quickly. Fluorescent lights making the halls too bright.

Room 115, and the door mostly closed.

I knocked softly and pushed it open. A curtain separated me from the rest of the room, and when I came around it—"Jay?"—he was there, lying on a high bed, not moving beneath still sheets, monitors rolled up beside him—like the others I'd seen.

His eyes were closed.

And that was it. That was it. Everything inside me came out.

Everything.

Joseph drowning in a pickup truck under the ice of the Alliance River.

Jupiter probably packing up and leaving us forever.

Brian Boss and Nick Porter following us. And now, look at what they'd done! Now look! Look at what they'd done!

I sat down on a plastic couch beside the high bed and bawled like anything, just bawled. I could hardly look at Jay Perkins. I could hardly look at his face, all swollen and battered and raw and bandaged. The hand that lay outside the sheets, stuck with an IV tube that dripped something clear into him. He took a breath, and paused. Took a breath, and paused. Every single time, it didn't sound like the next breath was a sure thing.

And he never moved.

And I wondered—stupid, I know—I wondered what happened to his dumb Mickey Mouse T-shirt.

I just wondered.

I'm not sure how long I bawled. Long enough for Ms. Uchida to come in, ask if there was anything she could do, then leave again when I shook my head.

And Jay still never moved.

I stood up beside the bed and leaned down toward him. "Jay Perkins. Jay Perkins," I whispered.

Nothing.

"Jay Perkins, I'm sorry for that time I smashed you into the lockers. I really am. I didn't get why you were so mad. And I guess I was pretty mad too. But that's over now, and you have to get better. Okay? You have to get better. I can't lose you. Okay? I can't lose you too. You know those times we run together? They mean a lot. A whole lot. More than just the running. More than that. I need you to run again—even if you wear that stupid Mickey Mouse T-shirt. Okay? I mean, I really really need you. And so does Jupiter. She needs you too. She needs you now more than ever, since they're going to take her away from us, and there will only be you to see her, since I don't think they're going to let me. There will only be you. And who else is going to tell me about her except for you? So Jay Perkins, Jay Perkins, you've got to wake up and get better. Okay? Okay?"

Nothing.

He never moved.

I was pretty snotty by then, but there was a box of tissues on the table beside the couch and I used a dozen or so. Maybe more. I stood by the bed for a while and watched him. I listened to his breath to be sure that the next one would come after the pause. Then a nurse came in and told me she was going to change his bandages and since it would take some time, perhaps—

"I'll come back tomorrow," I said.

"That would be nice."

"Will he know I'm here?"

"Hold his hand, then tell him you'll be here tomorrow," she said. "He'll know."

So I did. I took his hand and whispered, "Perkins, Perkins, Perkins, you jerk." I wanted more than anything for him to do something, anything, to let me know he heard.

But he didn't.

"Try again," said the nurse.

"Perkins," I said. "Jay Perkins. Jay goonie-pie."

Nothing.

"You can try again tomorrow," the nurse said.

I wasn't sure I could. It's hard to see nothing, when even just the tiniest little bit would mean everything.

Ms. Uchida stood up when I came into the waiting room. "Are you all right?" she said.

I nodded.

"I can take you back to school or I can take you home. Whichever one you want."

"Take me to the police station," I said.

And she did.

WE DIDN'T HEAR about Jupiter that day. Miss Canton called up after suppertime, and she said that was a good sign. It could have been an open-and-shut case, she said, but the fact that Judge Benedict was taking so long showed that she felt it was more complicated than just the straight facts would seem to indicate. "She said she was trying to think like a judge and like a brother," Miss Canton said. "I don't know what she meant."

My parents looked at me.

I shrugged, but that night, before I went to sleep, I stood by the open window and stared into the night, and I felt a little more hope than before that maybe, maybe Jupiter would always be just down the hall, quietly asleep, holding Affy-Giraffey and Solar the Polar Bear.

I really did feel that.

But I was wrong.

It's stupid to have hope.

It's always stupid—because things never work out like they're supposed to. Don't believe anyone who tells you they do. Don't believe anyone who tells you things are going to be all right. Because they aren't.

On Tuesday, Miss Canton called even before I was up.

I heard the phone ring in my parents' bedroom.

I heard them say hello to Miss Canton.

Then a long, long silence.

And that was that.

See what I mean?

I gave up.

My MOTHER DROVE me to see Jay Perkins after school that day. The desk attendant was different this time, and he asked if we were family, and I said yes, and he said, "Are you sure?" and

I said, "Do you think I'm lying, idiot?" (except I didn't say "idiot" out loud), and he said, "Five minutes. No more," and I went back to room 115.

Everything was pretty much the same, except that a long tube snaked down from a hookup in the wall and into Jay Perkins's nose. And he seemed paler, almost like he was taking on the color of the white sheets spread over him. Even his lips were paler, and his hands, and he was so still.

"Jay Perkins," I said. "Jay Perkins."

Nothing at all.

The pauses between his breaths were a lot longer.

I looked for a place to put my hand on him, but everywhere there were bandages and clear tubes.

"Jay, Coach Swieteck said to say hello. He told me to tell you that he figured you were slacking off, and he'd only give you a few more days before he'd be kicking your ass back to the track. He said you had to start thinking more about State than about lying around, okay? He said he didn't care how many broken bones you're supposed to have.

That's Coach, right? Always so hard-nosed but really . . ."

That was all I had in me to say. I stood by the side of the bed, listening to Jay Perkins breathe, until a nurse told me my time was up and I'd have to let Jay sleep.

"He's already asleep," I said.

"You might think so," she said, "but when someone comes in, he wakes up at least a little. I think he's more aware than you might imagine."

I looked at him. "Jay Perkins," I said, "this is from Jupiter"—and I leaned down and kissed him on the forehead.

ON THE WAY home, my mother turned on the local news to fill the silence in the car. First the weather, then the local traffic—as if there was any—and then news about the Sumner school district meeting last night. Then the announcement that two minors had been arrested in connection with the hit-and-run accident involving Jay

Perkins of East Sumner. Their names were being withheld pending further investigation.

"That certainly makes it sound like it wasn't an accident," said my mother.

We wound up Sumner Hill Road toward home.

"IN ORDER TO make the transition as easy as possible for Jupiter," Mrs. Stroud told us, "we have until the end of June. That way the Joyces can come several times to visit and get to know her. We want her to trust them and be ready to stay at home with them."

"Why should we want that?" I said.

"Jack," said my mother.

"I know this will be difficult for you, but you are going to have to let go," Mrs. Stroud said. "Jack, do you understand? You will have to let go. For her sake, Jack."

"I promised Joseph I would always know where she was."

"And you can keep that promise," Mrs. Stroud

said. "She'll be with her grandparents. She'll be with people who love her and who will care for her."

"That's not what I meant," I said.

"I know," said Mrs. Stroud. "But you're going to have to learn to mean it that way."

I knew I never would.

twelve

OST days now, I'd come home from school, change, and go run—four loops down Sumner Hill Road, through Jenny's Notch, across Mill Road along the Alliance River, then back up Sumner Hill Road. When I got home, I'd shower quick—I knew that Jupiter was waiting downstairs, and she stunk at waiting patiently—and then I'd put Jupiter on Marcus Aurelius and we'd head out to the Far Pasture, where the grass was growing high. She'd lean down from Marcus Aurelius's back, and I'd catch her and put her on the ground, and we'd hold hands and walk through the pasture. She would ask where Jay Perkins was and I would tell her he wasn't feeling well but he'd be back as soon as he could. She would nod and look around for something to pick. She would pick anything that was flowering and hold it tightly. Then I'd put her on my shoulders and carry her into the cool dark of the pine woods, and she'd hold on to my ears, and every so often she'd say, "Over there, Jackie," and she'd pick a pine cone off a branch. And when she had enough flowers and pine cones, we'd walk to the granite ledges and look down to where her father was asleep with the family, and I'd tell her about how Joseph used to stand by the window in the freezing cold in only his boxers and watch the planet Jupiter, and how he loved to milk Rosie even though he wasn't very good at it, and how he was smart in math and how he loved to read about Octavian Nothing and someday I'd read her that book but not right now.

How he missed her like anything.

She'd be quiet as she listened. Sometimes she'd lay her head against the back of my neck.

And then we'd both get on Marcus Aurelius and head home, and my mother would put Jupiter's flowers in a vase along with the flowers from the day before, and Jupiter would put the pine cones in a wooden box my father had brought into the kitchen for her collection, and then we'd go read or play blocks until my father would tell me he was ready to go, and the two of us would get in the pickup and drive to the hospital, where he would drop me off to see Jay Perkins.

For more than a week, Jay never said a thing.

He kept getting quieter and stiller and paler.

He lay in that high bed, beneath still sheets, monitors rolled up beside him. Eyes closed. Oxygen tubes up his nose. Face looking a little better, but still battered and bandaged. His hand still outside the sheets, stuck with the IV tube.

Those terrible long pauses between his breaths.

Not moving.

Once I met his father there.

I'd never seen him before, but they looked so much alike, you could tell right away who he was.

He was sitting on the couch, leaning forward, holding his hands in front of him like they were supposed to be doing something but he wasn't sure what.

"Who are you?" he said.

"Jack Hurd," I said.

He sat back. "Oh," he said. "You're the kid he ran with."

I nodded.

He looked down at his hands that still hadn't found something to do. "And you're the kid that Bennet and Judy are trying to take Jupiter from."

"Yeah," I said.

He leaned down, as if to look at his hands more closely. "I don't know if he's coming back," he said quietly.

"Who's coming back?"

"Jay."

"Mr. Perkins, he's right here."

"No, he's not. I don't know where he is, but he isn't right here." He stood and looked down at Jay. "And I don't know how to tell him how to come back. Or if he'd want to for me."

"Mr. Perkins—"

But he waved me off. "Have your visit," he said, and he started to walk out.

"Mr. Perkins, he's going to be all right."

He shook his head.

"Mr. Perkins, he is. He's going to be all right. We're all going to help him be all right."

Mr. Perkins turned and stood in the doorway. "How do . . . how do you know?"

"I just do," I said.

He looked at me for a long while, then turned and left.

That afternoon, I told Jay Perkins about running—that I was keeping up with four laps every day and five on Saturday and Sunday—and that there was a 10K over to Augusta at the end of July and maybe we could go together. I told him about Jupiter and her collection of pine cones and how she named one Jay because it sort of looked like his face. I told him about Coach Swieteck and how he was killing us with the Presidential Fitness Program he was probably just making up.

That sort of stuff.

He didn't move the whole time.

MOST VISITS, I didn't see anyone else in his room—until just a few days before we'd lose Jupiter. Then, when I walked into room 115, the Joyces were there, sitting on the couch.

They looked away from Jay Perkins when I walked in.

They looked at me.

They didn't look all that happy to see me. Especially Mr. Joyce.

I didn't care.

I walked over to Jay Perkins, leaned over him, and said, "Hey, Perkins, it's me."

"He won't hear you," said Mr. Joyce.

"He hears me," I said.

"How do you know?" said Mrs. Joyce.

"I can tell," I said.

Mrs. Joyce stood up and came beside me. "You are his good friend, aren't you, Jack?"

How are you supposed to answer something like that?

"He loved to run with you. He was such a good runner."

And then something happened that I never expected—and maybe I should have expected it, because of what Jay had told me about his uncle. But I didn't.

And at first, I didn't know what to do when it happened.

Mr. Joyce began to bawl.

It was horrible. Horrible. Big gulping howls— like he'd been trying to hold them in and now they were coming out and there was nothing he could do about it. Howl Howl Howl. His head in his hands, then his hands grasping at his chest as if he might explode. Mrs. Joyce went to sit beside him, and he shook his head because there was nothing he could do, nothing he could do, nothing.

I knew what this felt like.

"Jay," he said. "Jay, I'd give anything . . ."

I really did know what this felt like.

And maybe I shouldn't have, but how could I not? I crossed the room, sat down next to Mr. Joyce, put my arms around him, and held him.

"Jay," he said. "Maddie."

I held him tighter.

And here's where it doesn't help to tell you this story, because words don't always work. So if you can't get this part, there's nothing I can do about it. Because something went between us. Something like—I can't even describe it.

Understanding.

Maybe it was understanding that went between us.

Anyway, we sat there, the three of us, breathing kind of hard. Quiet. Listening to each other. And when I figured it was time to go, I let go and stood up, and Mr. Joyce looked at me, and he nodded, and I went over to Jay Perkins's bed and leaned over him.

He was so still.

I leaned down to Jay Perkins and I whispered, "Jay, you were right. Maybe he's not just a hard-ass." I took his hand—not the one with the IV tube—and I squeezed it hard. Real hard.

And you know what? Jay Perkins's eyes stayed closed—but they moved.

I swear they did.

They moved.

I looked back at Mr. and Mrs. Joyce. Then back at Jay Perkins. Then I hit the call button, like, twenty times.

"Hey, you jerk! Open your eyes!" I yelled.

Mr. and Mrs. Joyce stood up. "Jack," began Mrs. Joyce.

The nurse came in. "His eyes moved," I said.

"Are you sure?"

"I squeezed his hand and his eyes moved."

The nurse reached over and took his hand. "Jay," she said. "Can you hear me? Jay, wake up. Try to wake up."

"Hey, goonie-pie, open your eyes. Wake up.

Oh God, just open your damn eyes."

Mr. and Mrs. Joyce came to the bed.

"Jay," said Mr. Joyce.

And you know what?

You know what?

Jay Perkins opened his eyes. He did. He opened up first one, then both of his eyes.

"Jay, keep trying. Try to wake up," said the nurse.

Jay turned his head a little, looked at the nurse, looked at the Joyces, looked at me.

"That's it," the nurse said. "That's it."

Jay Perkins blinked. He tried to focus.

Then he spoke. "Not a goonie-pie," he said— and maybe it was slow, but it was loud and clear.

And Mr. Joyce began to bawl again.

THE NEXT DAY, Jay Perkins was loud and clear when he asked what happened to his Mickey Mouse T-shirt.

The next day, he was even louder and clearer

than before when he asked if Jupiter could come see him.

And the day after that, he might have been even louder and clearer, except that when Jupiter climbed on top of him, he had to hold everything in so he didn't holler brimstone and agony.

"You're going to be okay, you know," I said to him. "You'll be at State next fall."

"Standing watching," said Jay Perkins.

Right about then is when Jupiter bounced up and down on Jay's chest and he had to hold everything in.

I held everything in too, because when Jupiter did that, I knew she would always have her cousin. And he'd always have her.

Even if I wouldn't.

So THEN CAME Saturday.

In the last week, my mother and father had been trying to do what I couldn't do: get Jupiter ready for the idea that she'd be living with the Joyces from now on. They played with the stupid toys the Joyces left for Jupiter. They read the books the Joyces had brought. They looked at stupid pictures of the Joyces' big beautiful house and the big beautiful room that would be hers—Madeleine's old room. They talked about how nice Grandma was and how it was okay that sometimes Grandpa was a little grumpy—he was nice too.

Maybe they wanted me to help her get ready as well. But I couldn't. How could I? How could I tell her that everything she knew would be gone?

How could I tell her that we'd be gone?

I mean, she was only three. She wouldn't remember me when she grew older. She wouldn't know anything about Joseph. She wouldn't call me goonie-pie. She wouldn't ride on Marcus Aurelius's back. She wouldn't ask me to carry her into the pine woods. She wouldn't grab my ears and—

She wouldn't remember me.

She wouldn't remember me.

I imagined the awful quiet that would come into our house.

And I tried to think like a judge. I really did. But it was pretty hard not to hate Judge Benedict— even when I figured that the decision was probably brimstone and agony for her too.

Still, it was pretty hard not to hate her.

She probably knew that.

LITTLE BY LITTLE my mother packed Jupiter's things, even though Mrs. Stroud told her that Mrs. Joyce felt they were all set and didn't need anything from us. But my mother wanted Jupiter to have some familiar things around her "for the transition," and so she packed the clothes, and the blocks, and the books Jupiter loved—which meant finding every single Elephant & Piggie book in the house—and Affy-Giraffey, who got a bath and dried off while Jupiter sat in front of the dryer holding Solar the Polar Bear, waiting.

Friday had been awful, because everything was the last time. The last time we walked to the Far Pasture with her holding my ears, the last time we would eat supper together, the last time we read her books together, the last time she said, "Good night, Jackie goonie-pie," the last time I listened as she fell into that breathing that she did just before sleep—the last sleep in that room.

I lay awake all night, listening for any reason she might need me before Saturday came and I would break my promise and wouldn't know where she was anymore.

I listened as the cooling house settled its boards. I listened to an owl complain to the nighttime. I listened to a screech from a cat, probably, way up in the Far Pasture. I listened to the low hum of my parents talking in their bedroom, the ding of the woodstove as it cooled in the living room, the chime of the mantel clock at the quarter hour, at the half hour, at the three-quarters hour, at the full hour, as

Jupiter's last night with us sped away.

Then morning. I went downstairs and out to the Big Barn. Did chores. Came back inside. Sat at the kitchen table. Looked out at a rising sun. Waited.

Jupiter woke up. I heard my mother in her room, telling her she was going on a trip. With Grandma and Grandpa. Wouldn't that be exciting? No, we weren't going on the trip. No, Jackie wouldn't be going either. It was a trip for just Jupiter. We're packing all these things because you might need them on the trip. Yes, even the stocking cap that Jackie gave you. Let's be sure to put that in a special place. And all your books are downstairs by the back door so we won't forget them. What? No, Jupiter. We won't forget anything. We will never, ever forget anything.

Then my mother came downstairs with Jupiter, who was dressed like she was going to church.

"Jackie, can we go to the Big Barn?"

"You're all dressed up, Jupiter. You might get dirty."

"So?" said my father.

I looked at him.

"She's a farm kid. Let her be a farm kid while she can."

I picked Jupiter up and put her on my shoulders.

"Go ahead," said my mother, and Jupiter grabbed my ears, and we went into the Big Barn.

We scratched Rosie on her rump, because she loves that.

We groomed Marcus Aurelius, because he loves that.

We filled the bins with grain, even though I'd filled them earlier.

We shoveled out the manure, even though I'd done that too.

We climbed up into the hayloft and threw handfuls of hay at each other.

In the Small Barn, I pushed her on the rope swing, and she laughed and screeched like she never wanted to stop.

Neither did I.

And you know what? It turned out that for this day, we didn't have to.

Really.

My father called us inside. He leaned down and took Jupiter's hand. "Grandma and Grandpa aren't coming today," he said.

"They're not?"

"No, Jupe. Not today. Maybe tomorrow?"

"Can we go back to the swing?"

"If Jack isn't exhausted."

I looked at my mother. She shrugged. "Mrs. Stroud called," she said.

We went back to the swing.

One more day is one more day, and all that Saturday afternoon we played on the swing, and cleaned out stalls, and rode Marcus Aurelius well beyond the Far Pasture, Jupiter squealing as she held on to his rough mane.

Another call from Mrs. Stroud on Sunday, and Monday, and then Tuesday and Wednesday. "I don't know what they're thinking," Miss Canton told us.

"If they're going to take her," my father said, "they should damn well—"

My mother took his arm.

Thursday, then Friday.

Jay didn't know what they were thinking either.

I couldn't help but wonder if maybe—

FRIDAY AFTERNOON, COACH Swieteck sent a note during Music to tell me to meet him in his office after school. I guessed he wasn't interested in the problem of me missing the bus and having to walk home.

"I've got something for you to start doing," he said when I knocked and opened his office door.

"It's almost the end of school," I said.

He looked at me.

"Oh, right," I said.

He led me outside and we stood by the doors of the gym, looking down at the track, where there was a skinny kid running laps. You could tell even from here that he was wearing basketball shoes.

I watched for a while. "He runs like someone didn't put him together right," I said.

"Yeah, that's something you're going to have to deal with," said Coach Swieteck.

"Something *I'm* going to have to deal with?"

"His name is Petre. He's in fifth grade, and once he figures out that he doesn't have to run from side to side, he's going to be pretty good. He'll pick up a lot of time."

"Wait. I'm still back on 'something *I'm* going to have to deal with.'"

"This kid's from eastern Europe. Who knows where originally? No parents. The orphanage he was in was overcrowded times ten. He lay in his own piss for his whole first year, and it wasn't much better after that. He stayed there for eight years. You know how many kids die in their first eight years in places like that? Plenty. This kid made it. He's got hardly any school to talk about. His language skills stink, and not just in English.

He hasn't had a break his whole life—until now. Ms. Uchida has adopted him."

I watched the kid make his way around the track. He really did run side to side, and the way he held his hands up too high, and the way his head bobbled—

"You're going to run with him," said Coach.

"He's in sixth grade."

"And you're going to straighten that stride out. Bring his hands down. Build up his endurance. He's young, so you'll want to do most of this in the fields behind your house. Watch for signs of shin splints."

"Coach."

"You've got a few months before you're back with Perkins, and then it will be rehab for most of next year, I figure. You're going to have to set up some sort of schedule, since he's going to be living with his uncle and aunt now."

"He is?"

"That gives you time to get Petre up to speed.

If you two work at it, he'll be ready for middle school JV next fall."

"Okay."

Coach Swieteck looked at me. "Okay? Really? That was easier than I thought."

I shook my head. "No, it wasn't. You knew exactly what I was going to say."

Coach Swieteck smiled. "Yes, I did." He thumped me on the back. "Teachers really are like gods, aren't they?"

I headed down to the track.

THE NEXT DAY was Saturday, and I thought I might call Ms. Uchida to set up a running schedule for Petre. But that morning, a car drove in, and Mrs. Stroud got out. And Mrs. Joyce. And the whole world stopped—at least, for me.

Because it was about to happen.

Jupiter scrambled off the rope swing, fell, picked herself up, and ran out to them.

"Hello, precious," said Mrs. Stroud, and she leaned down to rub noses with Jupiter.

Mrs. Joyce held her arms out wide, and Jupiter ran into them, and Mrs. Joyce surrounded her.

"Jack," called Mrs. Stroud, "it's important that you stay here."

I ignored her.

I couldn't stay here. Not for this.

Not for this.

I went out to the Far Pasture, alone. I climbed down past the granite ledges, and I came into the family's graveyard. The day was quiet and a little bit cold, and the stones as I ran my hands over them still had some of last night's frost.

Except for Joseph's. His was always warm.

"I'm sorry," I said. "I'm so sorry. I am so sorry."

You can't believe how quiet it was among all those sleepers. It was like everything was stopped. Even the clouds looked like they were just painted on the sky, and the leaves held on for dear life. No sounds of birds. No squirrels running up and down the trees. No breath of wind to sway the pines.

I let myself slide down against Joseph's stone, and sat there with my back to it.

Nothing.

Nothing.

Nothing. For a long time, nothing.

And then Mrs. Stroud's car pulled up at the entrance to the graveyard, and Mrs. Joyce got out with Jupiter. Hand in hand, they came to Joseph's stone.

I stood.

"What are you doing, Jackie?" said Jupiter.

"Nothing," I said.

"I'm going to a McDonald's with a playground with Grandma."

"Okay," I tried to say. "Okay."

Jupiter knelt down to pull away the high grasses around Joseph's stone.

"Yes," said Mrs. Joyce. "We're going to a McDonald's with a playground. And then . . . we'll be back," said Mrs. Joyce.

I looked at her, and she smiled.

"Mr. Joyce and I had a long talk with Jay. A very long talk. And then we had another one. And another one. He's going to come live with us."

I nodded. "I know," I said.

"Jay has been a good friend to you, hasn't he?"

I nodded again.

"He's so much more grown up than I realized. And wiser than I ever knew."

"He's going to be okay," I said.

She nodded. "Yes, he is. Is that Joseph's stone?"

I moved aside so she could see it. She ran her hand along the top.

"It's so warm," she said.

Long silence.

"Mrs. Joyce," I said, "Joseph would have—"

"Jay told us that we should let Jupiter stay with you."

I put my hand on Joseph's stone, mostly to hold me up.

"He said that Jupiter is happy." Mrs. Joyce took a deep breath. She put both her hands on Joseph's stone. "He told us that Jupiter has a chance to grow up on a farm that she loves, and that she will grow up with a family she loves." Mrs. Joyce looked at Jupiter, then at me. "And with a family who loves her." Another deep breath. "He also said something about a robotics club, but I have no idea what he meant."

"It's okay," I said.

"And Jay said"—the deepest, longest breath of all—"Jay said that Madeleine would want Jupiter to stay with you."

Mrs. Joyce looked out over the three mountain ranges. The day was so clear, you could see the sharpness of each one of them, and you could imagine some painter sitting down and looking at those mountains and just giving up, since no one could copy the way they looked.

"And he said we should think about what's best for Jupiter, and not about what's best for us. And since then—since then, Mr. Joyce and I have done an awful lot of talking, and we wondered, if we had done that for Madeleine, maybe she would still—"

"It's not your fault," I whispered. "None of this is your fault."

Mrs. Joyce rubbed at her eyes. "And you," she said. "I hear you're going to be a judge someday."

"How do you know that?" I said.

"It seems that everybody knows that," she said, and then she put her hand to her mouth, and she began to cry.

Jupiter held her around her knees.

"Grandma crying?" said Jupiter.

"It's all right. It's all right," Mrs. Joyce said. "Everything is going to be all right." She picked Jupiter up. She held her tightly.

I waited.

"Jack," she said finally, "do you think you would mind very much if we came to visit now and then?"

THAT NIGHT, AFTER we finished reading a whole lot of Elephant & Piggie books, I straightened the blankets over Jupiter as she cuddled

Affy-Giraffey and Solar the Polar Bear into her arms.

"Is Jackie crying?" she said.

"Yes," I said.

"Are you sad?"

"No."

"Are you happy?"

I nodded.

"Why?"

"Because sometimes things work out like they're supposed to," I said. I took the books and stacked them beside her bed for tomorrow night. I leaned down close to her. "Don't believe anyone who tells you they don't. Don't believe anyone who tells you things aren't going to be all right. Because they are. Okay?"

"Okay, Jackie."

"Okay, Jupiter."

I tucked the blankets around her chin. She yawned, and closed her eyes, and nuzzled her head into the soft pillow. "Good night, Jackie goonie-pie," she whispered.

"Good night, Jupiter goonie-pie."

And I turned the light low, and kissed her good night, and rubbed her back as she smiled into sleep.